THE
DEPTFORD MICE
ALMANACK

THIS ALMANACK IS AN ACCOMPANIMENT TO:

THE DEPTFORD MICE TRILOGY:
THE DARK PORTAL
THE CRYSTAL PRISON
THE FINAL RECKONING

THE DEPTFORD HISTORIES:
THE ALCHYMIST'S CAT
THE OAKEN THRONE
THOMAS

Text and illustrations copyright © Robin Jarvis 1997

First published in Great Britain in 1997 by
Macdonald Young Books
an imprint of Wayland Publishers Ltd
61 Western Road
Hove
East Sussex
BN3 1JD

Designed by Chris Dymond, Triggerfish, Brighton

British Library Cataloguing in Publication Data available.
ISBN: 0 7500 2101 2

THE
DEPTFORD MICE ALMANACK

ROBIN JARVIS

MACDONALD YOUNG BOOKS

From the Sketchbook Journal of Gervase Brightkin

Once my only fear was that I might be engulfed by the collected material which this almanack contains. But now a very real dread sits by me. As I draw near to concluding my work, it is only too apparent that a new age of sorrow is dawning upon us. The blessed time is almost at an end and the chilling forces of night are mustering all around. May we all live through the sinister days ahead.

Permit me to introduce myself. I — Gervase Archibald Brightkin, of the red branch of squirrels, am the one responsible for this almanack — this hoard of eccentric and at times alarming lore and wisdom.

The respectable profession of travelling illuminator and recorder of likenesses is one in which I have been engaged for many years and in that time I have journeyed to many diverse lands. Yet few can match the shaded hillocks of this stately park wherein the Starwife dwells.

It is now three years since my return to Greenwich. When I was considerably greener behind the ears than I am now, I first stood upon that verdant, sweeping slope and demanded of the squeamish sentries to be taken to the old Handmaiden of Orion.

What a dragon that noble monarch was and how she terrified me with those milky eyes of hers which seemed to pierce my very soul. It was a very

Myself looking a trifle tubby

brief audience and she told me most impolitely to get out and never return until she had long gone to the Green.

I remember that at the time I was most offended, for I had offered to execute a portrait of her and perhaps restore her chambers back to their former glory, for they had been shockingly neglected and most of the ancient works were blackened with mould and caked with dust. But it was not permitted and so I left ~ with my tail very much between my legs.

Whilst the worthy baggage still lived I made it my business to keep away from that land and was too wrapped up with my various commissions to even think of it. Yet there came a day when I heard of the Starwife's passing and thought it was time to come and see for myself this new personage who had succeeded her.

The old Starwife

Well, I can only say that the present Handmaiden of Orion is less formidable than her predecessor, but when I saw her I was most startled. Since the beginning of days the office of Starwife was held by one of the five royal houses of black squirrels but not so today. She who now wears the silver acorn is none other than a mouse — and one of dubious background to boot!

Still, she has been good to me and I am now installed in two little rooms beneath the hill where I may work, for it is she who charged me — Gervase Archibald Brightkin, with the creation of something most vital and important. Within these pages I was commanded to set down, and illustrate where necessary, every date and festival of the slightest significance in the calendar — lest the future generations forget them.

It is a daunting task and sometimes I wish I had never accepted the work, for it grows with every hour.

The present Starwife, Audrey Scuttle as she appears now

At first I did think it would prove an easy feat, as I imagined that only the days in the squirrel year would be needed, but she has commanded that all folk must be represented. Thus have I journeyed to a desolate little spot called Fennywolde where Master William Scuttle dwells and to the great mouse realm of Holeborn in the City where Arthur Brown rules as Thane. Within these pages are set down the twilight doctrines of those mysterious creatures — the bats. There are also extracts taken from aged manuscripts stored deep below the observatory hill in the Starwife's archive chambers and samplings from various diaries and fragments of weather and herb lore, some of them gathered from the most unlikely sources.

Yet since this work was begun, it has taken a darker road than I anticipated. The uncouth and horrifying festivals of the rats are given their grim mention here and learning of their heinous rituals has coloured my

dreams with flames of war and drowned them in blood. But that is not why my heart mourns. A shadow of some dreadful darkness is closing about Greenwich and though I cannot discern why, this once cheerful, merry place has become filled with whispers of insurrection and deceit. I fear very strongly that this almanack may prove, in the end, to be a memorial of all that once was - before the great darkness came.

May the Green watch over us.

Gervase Brightkin

A Key to the Symbols Used in this Almanack

 Those customs and beliefs particular to mice

 Squirrel lore

 The insight of the bats

 Weather wisdom

 The ramblings of Madame Akkikuyu

 Concerning the alchemist Dr Elias Theophrastus Spittle

 The misguided creed of pagan ratfolk

 According to Thomas Triton

 Personal thoughts and opinions of Gervase Archibald Brightkin

JANUARY

JANUARY

1 On this, the first day of the year, all creatures are sure to take great note of the first folk to cross their threshold. The nature of this important guest will determine the fortune for the rest of the year. It should be noted however that today is a great opportunity for mischief and, in some areas, rats will purposely go a knocking extra early in order 'to spoil the luck'. If they are not pelted with stones or beaten with sticks on sight, these first, unwanted visitors might also gobble up the unsuspecting host.

2
The Day of the Fir
The merriest of the five royal houses of black squirrels were those of the Fir. Their badge was the fir cone and their queen wore one wrought of gold about her neck. Of all creatures they were said to be most skilled in the art of music and could lull their enemies to sleep by its power. The Fir realm was eventually destroyed from within and so this day is set aside to remember them.

3 Audrey Scuttle (née Brown), the sister of Arthur, was born this day to Gwen and Albert in the Skirtings. Of all mice she is held in the highest esteem, for it was she who rid the world of Jupiter's unholy menace. Now, Audrey sits upon the Living Throne in Greenwich as the Starwife where she has reigned wisely for over ten years.

JANUARY

4  The first full moon of the new year is a revered time for all bats. This is the time when important new prophecies are made.

Bats are very curious and most irritating. Most of their prophecies are couched in the form of riddles and by the time you have worked out what they mean, the forecasted event has already happened.

---

5  **From the writings of the alchemist Dr Elias Theophrastus Spittle:**
The gemstone associated to this pernicious, benighted month is the Garnet which signifies truth and fidelity and is reputed to clear confusion in the mind.

Yet I abhor to see others content and so at times, to ease the trial of witnessing their silly smiling faces, I prepare a minor poison and sprinkle it over the wares of the grocer or fishmonger and have been most gratified to hear the moans of the vomiting sickness continue well into the night from neighbouring dwellings.

---

6 Snorri, a Norwegian mariner mouse arrived in the city of Hara in the year of Jupiter's downfall and was given seven small wooden carvings by the holy Sadhu which he later brought to Greenwich and traded with Kempe.

7 Tonight the Starwife bade me leave my quarters and wait at a desolate, dismal spot down by the railings.

With a quaking heart I obeyed and stood, trembling, in the darkness when suddenly, a cracked voice called out from the gloom. It was the voice of a rat!

But I need not have worried, for it was only old Dodder, a harmless fellow who had never had any dealings with Jupiter's unholy crew. He has sworn to relate all I need about those rituals and ceremonies important to his barbaric kin so that I may complete this commission, though insists on doing so in secret, as "the big rules is forbid to them's not born in the blood". The interview was curtailed abruptly when a noise startled him and he disappeared into the night.

8 *Now is the time for all mice to prepare for the coming festivity of Yule. Cakes and biscuits must be made and the fine ale brought out of storage to wash down the chestnuts which are to be roasted.*

9 **YULE** *The first of the three days of the festival of Yule begins. The time when the Midwinter Death seems to press His closest. This is a cosy day for sitting around the fire, telling ghostly tales. The late tutor of the Skirtings, Master Oldnose, would always try to invent haunting yarns but they were never very popular, especially 'Bohart and the friendly moon spirits' which every child had heard umpteen times apparently. When the Starwife related this ludicrous nonsense to me, I could see why. The fellow may have been a fine mousebrass maker, but his imagination was severely lacking.*

10 **YULE** *In these days of Yule it is important to eat as much as possible to survive the coming hardship that the winter brings. It was upon this night that the bats left Deptford to go to their great meeting in the dome of Saint Paul's.*

11 **YULE** *The final day of the Yule festival. A time to both reflect and look forward. On this day Piccadilly met Barker in the Underground and learned the disquieting news of the growing unrest in the City's rats.*

JANUARY

12 This was when Piccadilly and his hapless friend Marty secretly observed the Ratmoot and discovered that the new leader 'Old Stumpy' was none other than Morgan, Jupiter's old lieutenant. That same day Holeborn was attacked and every mouse was killed.

13 The year after his body was destroyed, the terrible spirit of Jupiter rose to assail Greenwich and stole the mighty Starglass. Having journeyed to Deptford with Thomas Triton, the old Starwife lit a beacon fire to summon the bats. Yet when they came, Orfeo and Eldritch took Oswald to their council instead.

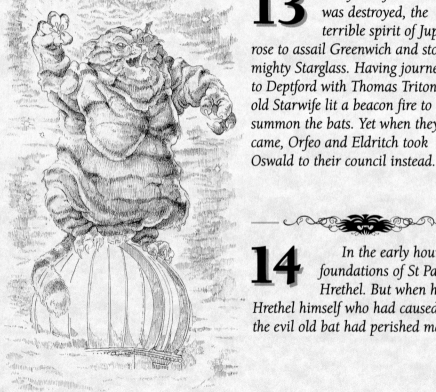

14 In the early hours Oswald Chitter was sent below the foundations of St Paul's Cathedral to discover the Great Book of Hrethel. But when he succeeded he was cheated at the last by Hrethel himself who had caused the writing to disappear from the pages before the evil old bat had perished many years ago.

JANUARY

15 Using the power of the Starglass, this was the night that Jupiter stole the starlight from the heavens.

16 After the slaughter in Holeborn, Jupiter appeared to his old lieutenant, Morgan, and so ensnared him into his service once more.

17 That night, Piccadilly battled against Jupiter's old lieutenant but, realising he would never be free of Jupiter's control, Morgan finally killed himself. Piccadilly was also slain and Audrey Scuttle was tricked by the old Starwife into accepting the silver acorn.

18 *The Day of Deliverance*
This day will always be renowned as the time when Jupiter was utterly vanquished. His reborn spirit was sent hurtling through the heavens – to be eternally consumed by the unstoppable agonies of unending life.

There was great joy, and the Green Mouse himself appeared, yet it was also tempered with sadness, for the old Starwife had perished and Oswald Chitter had been lost in the eternal void – beyond the living plane.

19   *According to the various seafaring folk, there were rumours that pieces of the shattered Starglass fell all over the world today.*

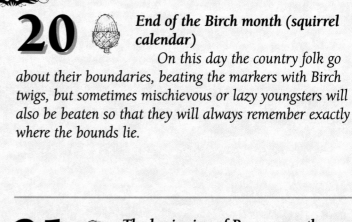

20   **End of the Birch month (squirrel calendar)**

On this day the country folk go about their boundaries, beating the markers with Birch twigs, but sometimes mischievous or lazy youngsters will also be beaten so that they will always remember exactly where the bounds lie.

21   **The beginning of Rowan month (squirrel calendar)**

In ancient times the squirrels would bury their slain enemies with a Rowan stake through the heart to prevent their ghosts from returning to haunt them. Yet in this month garlands are still made from Rowan twigs and brought into the home where they are placed above the doors to keep out any unwelcome or sinister visitor.

JANUARY

22 On this day in 1665 the alchemist Dr Elias Theophrastus Spittle went to the raghouse and discovered the heavily embroidered robe of Magnus Zachaire, which contained more secrets than he ever came to realise.

23 On this night Dr Elias Theophrastus Spittle took Will Godwin and the kitten Jupiter to the churchyard of St Annes where he summoned the spirit of Magnus Augustus Zachaire and imprisoned it within a bottle.

24  The night the bats honour Rohgar, the most famous and fiercest of their generals. Every weaning yearns to become as fearless as this renowned Moonrider.

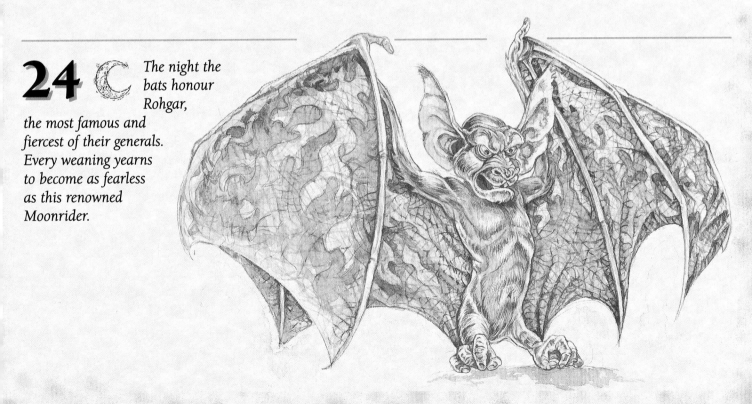

JANUARY

25

Today that toadying attendant to the Starwife, Fitz, came into my quarters to inquire how the almanack was progressing. I promptly told the young slywhiskers that it was nowhere near completed and only just begun. Fitz was most vexed and stormed off huffily. Pries into every corner, that one, I don't trust him one tiny bit. Even now he is probably tittle-tattling some spiteful tale about me. Well, I'm too busy to fret about his petulant tongue.

26

Cats have their own beliefs and few of us have ever conversed with one long enough for this knowledge to amount to very much. I shall however try to set down all that is known of 'The Hunter's Creed', beginning with the most fundamental law which they teach their kittens in these times of cold, deep nights. In the shadows there waits one who will claim them all in the end and the whole of their lives is a contest to keep 'He that walks in darkness' at bay.

27

A map of Greenwich and its environs, marking some of the sites mentioned in this almanack.

A *The observatory hill wherein the Starwife dwells*
B *The Great Oak*
C *Blackheath*
D *The Cutty Sark*
E *The River Thames*

28

Ten years ago today Arthur Brown led a large company of fellow mice from the Cutty Sark to seek out the realm of Holeborn, where his late friend Piccadilly had lived. Whereas most of those he left behind have forever afterwards called this 'The Great Desertion', Arthur eventually became the Thane and governs the City still.

JANUARY

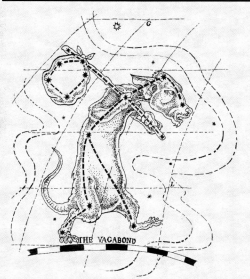

THE VAGABOND

29

The Bauchanite moon enters the sign of the 'Vagabond' (Rat Zodiac)

The rat born at this time is a malcontent who either leaves his birthplace because of a burning lust to spy other realms and darker holes, or is driven out because of some crime. Thereafter the 'Flearunner', 'None-to-mourn' or 'Stinkheel' as he is vulgarly known will be a loner doomed to traipse the world for ever.

Infamous Flearunners include: Madame Akkikuyu Heliodorus

30

From the writings of the alchemist, Doctor Elias Theophrastus Spittle:

How well doth I remember this day in 1649, for the sovereign Charles was beheaded outside the Banqueting Hall of Whitehall.

'Twas a most pleasing display and I succeeded in mine ambition. Even now I hold the glass phial in my hand which still contains the royal blood I harvested upon that day, for that which fuels the veins of a sovereign is most precious in the art of sorcery.

31

As the beliefs of all other races and creatures are to be set down here I see no reason why my own should be neglected. Henceforth I shall periodically describe that which has had the most profound influence throughout my life – the force and nature of colour.

BLACK

Mostly associated with death and mourning, this is the shade of night under whose ebony cloak untold horrors may tread. Yet it is also the tint of the fur which sets apart the five royal houses of the squirrels. Now departed from this world, they were the wisest and most noble of all and their like shall never been seen again.

FEBRUARY

FEBRUARY

1  Heed the weather of this month, for according to Old Todmore of Fennywolde.

If February give much snow,
A fine summer it do foreshow.

2 In this season of long, dark nights, it is prudent to lay in a good store of candles. In every community there is normally one 'Wickster' whose task this is. It is an important position, for it is widely believed that candle flames drive away the spirits of the cold which roam the freezing darkness seeking for the unwary. Many traditions have grown up around the role of the 'Wickster', it is he who symbolically keeps the ember of hope alive and no other may light the Yule fire which sees everyone through the darkest nights.

 **3** To ease the sniffles which invariably arrive in this wet season, take a quantity of orange and lemon rind, boil it in a pot of water with a pinch of cinnamon then stir in a good dollop of honey, strain and sip.

This basic recipe has many variants, I have heard of garlic being added to the drink, but the most sick-making must be the special ingredient favoured by Madame Akkikuyu. **The fortune-telling rat swore by the addition of a live frog to the brew, which then had to be boiled till 'the juicey it leaks and makes it thick like phlegm'.**

FEBRUARY

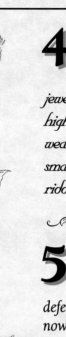

4

From the writings of the alchemist Dr Elias Theophrastus Spittle:

The Amethyst dost this month proclaim as its own. Tis a fair jewel, yet worth little, save amongst the heathen who reserve its use for their high priests to adorn their ceremonial knives. Yet tis also said to protect the wearer from drunkeness and that old trollop, Peggy Blister, did purchase a small bauble of Amethyst on learning this intelligence. Would that all her pox ridden, tippling patrons at The Sickle Moon were of like mind.

5

When the first Snowdrop emerges above the soil in Greenwich, the squirrels give thanks, for such a flower appeared in the ashes of the old Starwife's pyre and, with its aid, Audrey Scuttle was able to defeat the spirit of Jupiter. It is said by my grey cousins hereabouts that nowhere are the snowdrops more lovely than here and they perceive it as a sign that the old Starwife is still watching over them.

6

The day when Bib, one of the Landings mice ventured into the cellar never to return. His peeled skin was later discovered by Piccadilly and Oswald in Morgan's revolting treasure store and larder.

7

Tonight I had a message from Dodder, the rat informant, and quickly ran down the hill to meet him. He was less nervy this time and I half filled my pad with notes — the things those rat folk believe!

8 This is the season when foxes court their mates. But what a racket they make and what little regard they show for decorum or the sensibilities of others.

9 The day that Morgan, the young, piebald, Cornish rat first entered the sewers at Deptford and was taken to see the altar of Jupiter. In those days Jupiter's lieutenant was Black Ratchet, a devious creature who was nearing the end of his usefulness. Already there was talk of mutiny against him, but Jupiter protected the rat until a suitable replacement could be found. Even on that first encounter it is said that he noticed Morgan's potential.

10 ⚓ According to Thomas Triton, in these days of storm and bad weather, to calm a tempest, cast a coin into the wind to propitiate the sea nymphs and Lords of the Deep.

Whilst interviewing the midshipmouse for the purposes of this almanack it became increasingly apparent that he was too fond of his rum and at one point began singing to himself. I do not think I like Mr Triton very much. Most of what he has told me, including his history, I have found impossible to believe, but one thing was made very plain throughout the course of our discussions — he truly is an expert on the subject of wind!

11 ☾ The Moon's Phases as viewed by her subjects, the bats.

Blind She

Her Power Waning

Lady Waking

Watchful Glory

FEBRUARY

12 The day when crave lures or hanker dolls are popular with lusty rat maidens who have had no success in catching the eye of the one they favour. These crudely made effigies are sewn from scraps of cloth and rag. Stuffed with herbs, purchased from the likes of Madame Akkikuyu, bacon rind and fur slyly plucked from the objects of their desire, they are then stitched with whiskers and worn about the neck until the longed for mate is captured either by the charm's power or the smell of the bacon rind.

13 At this time of year, when the moon is waxing, the young bats – or weanings – leave their families and begin their training to become Knights of the Moon. Not every bat is suited or even able to complete the rigorous tests they must undergo and those who failed were only permitted to collect the eggs used in the making of pouch bombs.

Although the need for fire eggs has long since passed, training is still just as thorough and it begins with the weanings learning the complicated and mysterious history of their race.

14 Now that the days are becoming longer, the hazards of life in the country ease a little. Fuel and food may be gathered more leisurely without the constant fear of an attack by a marauding owl.

15 *Clatter Day*
In Fennywolde at this time the mice will walk across the fields whilst making as much noise as possible, banging pots and pans together and playing raucous tunes to awaken the sleeping land spirits, calling on them to bless the soil and make the crops of the coming year grow tall and plentiful.

16

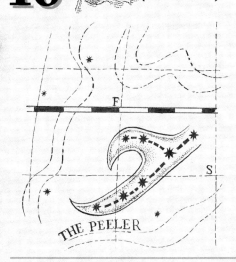

The moon leaves the house of Bauchan and enters that of Hobb with the sign of the Peeler (Rat Zodiac)

Surely the most respected of all constellations, it has many other vulgar names: 'Gutgorer', 'Flabripper', 'Bloodspike', 'Lardshaver', 'Giblet-render' and 'Furtrimmer'. The rat born now will never want for fresh meat – be it mouse or mole, stoat or weasel. They are expert hunters and can skilfully skin the hide off the most unwilling of prey in a trice. Such is the pride a rat will take in this birthsign that he will often cut off one of his claws at the wrist and replace it with a sharpened knife to make his peeling even more efficient.

Infamous Gutgorers include: *Skinner*

Wendel Maculatum, the stoat, was also born at this time.

THE PEELER

17

The last day of the Rowan month (squirrel calendar)
Be sure to remove all Rowan garlands, for to keep them indoors once the month is over will bring disastrous ill fortune.

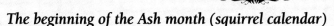

18

The beginning of the Ash month (squirrel calendar)
Known as 'the strangling tree' because its roots will suffer no competition from others, the Ash is not loved by squirrels and they make no celebration this day. Yet by other creatures it is credited with many powers. Rats will pass their newborn young through a cleft in the branches as it is supposed to make them hale and tenacious fighters. Mariners value its wood which they believe protects them from drowning and shrews believe it guards them from snakes.

19

Piccadilly was born on this day, a year before Arthur and Audrey Brown. Orphaned at a very young age, the citymouse did not believe in the spirit of the Green and preferred instead to depend upon his own sharp wits. One of the finest foragers in the immense mouse realm of Holeborn, Piccadilly eventually found himself in Deptford where he became embroiled in the desperate struggle with the rat god Jupiter in which he lost his life.

As I questioned the present Starwife about Piccadilly, her eyes became filled with sorrow and when she saw the drawings of him which I have drafted from the various descriptions I have heard, she could not speak and rushed quickly away. But, when she recovered, the Starwife requested the largest of the paintings for herself and it now hangs behind the Living Throne.

20

The sign of Hope which belonged to Piccadilly. Closely linked with the sign of Life, this is meant to inspire the bearer unto great deeds and surmount adversities and hardship.

21

 *A dangerous day for all enemies of rats. This is the time of First Blood, when those ratlings who have not yet committed murder must do so before the moon sets in the sky and bathe in their victim's crimson juices. If a ratling returns without a drop of blood on him then he is shamed and will not live long, for others will make it their business to 'spike' him.*

FEBRUARY

22

The greenish yellow catkins should now be appearing upon the Hazel tree. As the Hazel is the symbol of wisdom, it is the custom for youngsters who are falling behind in lessons and getting sore paws as a result, to bring a spray of catkins into their bedchamber in the hope that they will grow wiser as they sleep.

23

Today the Starwife sent one of her attendants to my quarters. Ambrose is not so fawning as Eitz, his counterpart, but is always eager to advance himself. To aid me in my work, I have been commanded to visit Holeborn to interview the Thane about his role in that desperate time. It is not a journey I relish for it will mean travelling via the sewers.

24

The frightful helm, 'Warbrow', worn by the moonrider Aldwulf who fought in the great battle at the Hallowed Oak against the children of the Raith Sidhe.

FEBRUARY

25 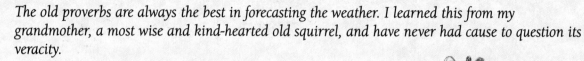 *The old proverbs are always the best in forecasting the weather. I learned this from my grandmother, a most wise and kind-hearted old squirrel, and have never had cause to question its veracity.*

If early morning your whiskers itch, by noon there'll be a flooded ditch.

26 This day in Fennywolde the fieldmice decide who will be their King of the Field for the coming year. Since the death of Mr Woodruffe, William Scuttle has won every time, despite fierce competition from Figgy Bottom.

The burial mound of Mr Woodruffe

27  ### VIOLET

Most useful for depicting the deep shadows of winter, as the flower of the same name is now coming into bloom, it seems appropriate to place this colour here. There are those in Fennywolde who believe that to bring less than a pawful of violets indoors is most unlucky, and I would agree with this, simply because I adore to sugar and consume the petals of this delicious plant.

28 ### Extract from the travelling journal of Gervase Brightkin - Day 1

Today I set off from Greenwich to journey to Holeborn with messages of goodwill from the Starwife to her brother, Arthur — the Thane. I can only pray that the sewers when I enter them are as safe as they have been all these years since Jupiter's demise.

29

As this day only occurs once every four years it is considered very special. Shrews, who never like anything unexpected, view the extra day and anything they meet during it, as suspicious and will not talk to any stranger until March commences.

Stoats however see things differently. As the next twenty-ninth of February won't come along for a while, they make up for it by eating an extra three days' worth of food. It is a common sight to see stoats rolling around at this time, fit to bursting – those animals who have managed to squeeze through the entrance to their homes, that is.

Mice and squirrels however see this as a time of romance and maidens with reluctant or shy admirers will often make the first move upon this day. Many are the weddings I have attended that have been the result of a Leap Day.

MARCH

❧ MARCH ❧

1 An excellent day to sow beans – but beware. The scent of the flowering broad bean induces dreams and the Rat Priestesses of Mabb, the sleep visitor, would often spend the night in a beanfield to experience her ghastly nightmares. Ordinary rats used Mabb Rests, sacking pillows stuffed with these flowers and herbs, to commune with the terrifying consort of Hobb.

2 This is the month when hares are to be seen leaping and dancing in the fields. This is in honour of The Ancient, the moon-sent angel who came to earth in the form of a hare to commune with every night-loving creature. Legend says that this revered entity still lives deep below the earth and when the time of the direst need approaches he will emerge and battle with Hobb himself.

3 *Extract from the travelling journal of Gervase Brightkin – Day 4*

My fourth day in the sewers. This is quite the foulest place I have ever had the misfortune to see. I can only wonder what hungry eyes are glaring at me from the surrounding blackness. Every now and then I pause in my tracks to glance at the map (I pray that Triton was sober when he drew it) and judge that the vast realm of Holeborn cannot be much further. The very thought of the evil deeds which were committed down here sit heavily upon my spirits. I half expect to stumble across a pile of old chewed bones — well, better that than fresh ones I suppose.

MARCH

4 Traditionally, this was the day that the first earthly manifestation of Suruth Scarophion was vanquished upon the very steps of the original black temple. Of those present all those ages ago, Simoon the prophet still lives. But where he is now, no one – not even the bats know.

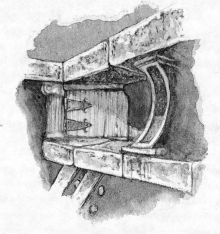

5 The repaired entrance to Holeborn.

6 On wet mornings at this time of year, earthworms come wriggling to the surface so it is a common and comical sight to see one or more moles scurry from their hills to find as many of these squirming dainties as possible.

7 **From the writings of the alchemist Dr Elias Theophrastus Spittle:**

This is the month of the Bloodstone, that which purports to bring valour unto he who possesses it. Tis yet another falsehood, for I durst put it to the test. In the dead of night I did stride forth in the hope of meeting adventure and tempering my natural craven nature. But I did journey only a few yards when terrible howls afflicted my ears. Like the release of untold demons from Hades the screams did surround me and I did flee homeward as swiftly as I could gallop. Yet twas merely Verney the Adamite, he of that ridiculous and breezy sect which believed that mankind should return to its original unclad state. Twould appear he has fallen back into his old loony humours again and was alarming the geese and other fowl with his nakedness as he lurched through the streets pursued by the Captain of the Watch.

❧ MARCH ❧

8 In the early March sunshine it is just as well to recall the old saying,

Only when you can lie upon nine daisies is it Spring.

9 ### The Fennywolde games

This day is set aside for the fieldmice to find a champion who will be given the grave responsibility of head sentry for the whole of the summer. Many feats of agility and endurance are performed today; stalk climbing, ditch leaping, bramble vaulting, stone hurling and the-pool-and-back race, are but a few of them.

10 Now do the bat weanings take to the night air for the first time. Eventually when the youngsters become more skilled, two wren's eggs will be placed in a pouch to be worn around the weaning's neck and only when seven flights of complicated manoeuvres are completed with no damage to the shells are they considered to be of an adequate standard.

11 This mousebrass is becoming increasingly popular in the cities, as foxes (or 'Brush Buttocks', as Twit called them) spread into the urban areas.

The Anti-Fox charm.

❧ MARCH ❧

12 The moon enters the sign of the Bloodybones (Rat Zodiac)

At certain times, the most feared of the Raith Sidhe would appear to his 'children', and walk amongst them stripped of all flesh. Thus have his high priests always arrayed themselves in costumes which emulate this state. A rat born at this time may devote himself to the worship of those filthy gods and aspire to attaining the powerful position of high priest. The other, main purpose of the bloodybones costume is disguise, for the identity of the high priest has ever been cloaked in secrecy.

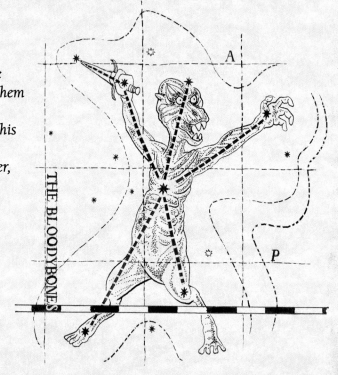

THE BLOODYBONES

13 Extract from the travelling journal of Gervase Brightkin – Day 14

I have been in Holeborn nearly a fortnight now and have learned all I can from Arthur Brown, the Thane. He and the mice who dwell here have laboured long to repair the damage wrought by Morgan and his army of city rats in that dreadful time. Yet I yearn for the sunlight and this very afternoon am leaving for home.

14

As well as being beautiful and fearfully difficult to paint successfully, rainbows are always excellent indicators of the coming weather. Old Todmore says of them:

If there be a rainbow in the eve,
twill rain and leave:
But if there be a rainbow in the morrow,
twill neither lend nor borrow.

MARCH

15

The day that Morgan, in his youth, throttled Black Ratchet his predecessor and became Jupiter's new lieutenant.

16

Extract from the travelling journal of Gervase Brightkin - Day 17

The return journey to Greenwich was uneventful, apart from a frightful experience when I fell through a moss-covered crevice in the brickwork. How I yelped with fear! The place I had accidentally discovered was a pagan rat temple, dedicated to the Raith Sidhe and upon one of the three altars was the headless skeleton of a rat. The vile spot should be destroyed — it makes my fur prickle to think about what might have occurred down there.

17

The end of the Ash month (squirrel calendar)
Upon this night the hosts of Hrethel attacked the fair realm of Greenreach with their dreaded pouch bombs and Morwenna, whose name is forever accursed, slew the Starwife.

18

The beginning of the Alder month (squirrel calendar)
Formerly known as Aldertide, this was once a time of great celebration, when high revels were held. But the Hazel Realm of Coll Regalis was destroyed by the bats upon this day long centuries ago and so Aldertide is no longer observed. Instead it is a solemn occasion when it is well to consider the folly of war and attempt to patch up old quarrels.

19 This was the time the Lady Ysabelle and Vesper escaped from the Hobbers, but not before the high priest had awakened Hobb from his eternal rest with the aid of the Silver Acorn.

There is an old rhyme about the worshippers of the Raith Sidhe, which runs:

> **Tread not into the fearsome night**
> **But pull the covers high,**
> **Step not into the wild dark wood**
> **For the Hobbers are dancing nigh.**

Hobb lantern

20 On this day Vesper and Ysabelle met Giraldus, the leprous mole, and his servant Tysle – the lame shrew. During the night, the spirit of the Green appeared to Ysabelle and gave her hope in her quest.

21 Ysabelle and the others were reunited with Wendel Maculatum this day, who led them to the mournful lake where Vesper was almost dragged to his doom by the unnatural creatures of the dark water.

22 The day when Ysabelle's company met Fenlyn Purfote and were granted an audience with the Ancient. Then was Wendel revealed to be the high priest of Hobb and both Tysle and Giraldus lost their lives. At the close of the day Hobb erupted from the earth at Greenreach but was imprisoned within an acorn by the power of the Starglass and the Hallowed Oak was felled.

23 When the bats finally learned from Vesper of Hrethel's greed and deceit, they laid seige to his stronghold upon this day. But the evil Warden of the Great Book refused to surrender and his coveted treasure was not retrieved until the arrival of Oswald Chitter many hundreds of years later.

24 Now should all birds guard their eggs, for rats are not the only ones fond of these delicacies. In days of old, bats would steal them in order to make their much feared pouch bombs.

Thomas Triton insists that it is most important to break the shell of an egg after it has been eaten to prevent ships from being wrecked — really that midshipmouse becomes more embarrassing with each new day.

symbol of the fire eggs

❧ MARCH ☙

25

The feast day of Wilfrid, the first mouse smith who was taught by the Green Mouse himself to make the earliest brasses in the deeps of legend. From this ancient time every sign and charm can be traced and the mice celebrate it by singing the song of 'Wilfrid the maker' and Master Walter Thistlewick and his lads dance the traditional 'Looping the Brass'.

Wilfrid's brass

26 **Dandelions now flowering at the wayside**

Also known as wet-the-beds, these are most useful blooms. The leaves are, I have been told, quite pleasant to eat and the bright yellow petals make a wonderful dye which is commonly used in the quilt making of the winter months. I believe also that there are those who make wine from the plant but then some fellows (mentioning no names) will drink practically anything.

27 In this season the furze, or gorse, is flowering to feed the first bees. Go to a hive this night and press an ear against it, for the occupants are said to hum Green psalms to bring about the warmer weather.

28

A sure sign that the recipient will never be content to remain anywhere for long. Thomas Triton bears one of these, as did Madame Akkikuyu who received it in payment from one of her clients many years ago.

The sign of the Travelling Mouse

29

Taken from the Diary of Walter Thistlewick:

As squire of the Skirting's Morris and Sword Dancers, I led my seven hale and hearty lads in the tradishunal March display of 'Dancing the Fool'. Beecoz Herbert Chickweed's got a broke leg, young Freddy Beechnut took his place. Oh but he was real awful, the fat, gormless lump – cuddent rember the steps an cracked poor Percy Bobbin on the noggin four times with his tiddling wand. To top it all, the bells which should've been tied round his elbows, fell off and us all slipped. I've never been so humilihated, we was each on our backsides – save him still waving his arms about like a big daft ninny.

30

A grim anniversary. In the dead of night, when Albert Brown was just a child, thirty bloodthirsty rats squirmed through the Grill. Taken unawares and completely defenceless, fifteen mice were butchered and twenty-two more were carried off to a hideous doom in the sewers. Upon the Cutty Sark and in Holeborn, they still remember this outrage and commemorate it by tying a black ribbon about their tails.

31

According to Old Todmore now is the time to tally up the number of mists seen in this month to forecast the weather in May, for the proverb says:

So many mists as fogs the eyes in March,
as many frosts to snap the whiskers in May.

APRIL

❧ APRIL ❧

1 ⚓ According to Thomas Triton, an idiot or simpleton is one of the few folk a seafarer is pleased to meet when embarking upon a voyage, as this is seen as a fortunate omen.

   If that was indeed the case (and I doubt it, for the rum was flowing very freely when he told me this) then I can only imagine that he was one of the most popular fellows on board ship!

2 As this month is prone to showers it is well to recall a favourite saying of Old Todmore, the fieldmouse – a fount of all country lore:

After rain comes sunshine.

3 'Terrorgrin' – the screechmask of Vesper's father.

APRIL

4  **The Day of Keys**

This month and the next are said to be the keys of the year so this day is a time for the secrets or troublesome thoughts which burden the heart to be revealed and laid bare. In the past it was also a time to leave the door unbolted and welcome any stranger to come into the nest to share the evening meal, but these days this custom is no longer observed for there are far too many peculiar and dangerous folk abroad.

5  Hedgehogs are now up and about after their winter sleep. These fellows are inquisitive beyond measure and will engage you in conversation for the entire day if you permit it.

Only yesterday I was out with the intention of making a study of the Great Oak, when old prickles came lumbering from the gorse. Needless to say, the drawing of the Oak was never completed and I was compelled to sketch my new aquaintance, Pirkin Gim-Gim, instead. I do hope he does not turn up at my quarters as he promised, or this almanack shall never be finished.

6  **From the writings of the alchemist Dr Elias Theophrastus Spittle: 1665**

This night I did see a bright comet blazing in the heavens. 'Tis surely a portent of some great evil which is to befall us. I have consulted my charts and do conclude that Death is very near and shall shortly dance his macabre jig throughout this city leading many with him. A shadow has seized my heart and I shall seek my bed early.

7 A great celebration day for the fieldmice of Fennywolde. According to tradition, this is when Fenlyn Purfote arrived in this land with his followers and claimed it in the name of those woodlanders displaced by the evil forces of Hobb.

8 One of the rarest mousebrasses, this is a much yearned for sign by those girl mice who are inclined to be vain and wish to be recognised for their looks alone. The symbol of Beauty, it has been known to turn the bearer's head completely and utterly spoil her previous pleasant nature, as was the case with Alison Sedge.

The sign of Grace and Beauty

9 This month is sacred to the Lady of the Moon. If she is full in the sky upon this night there is great rejoicing amongst the bats who ride beneath her singing an endless melody in praise.

10 Trees are now budding with new leaves, and according to Old Todmore there is a sure way of forecasting the coming summer:

> **Oak before ash**
> **Twill be but a splash**
> **Ash before Oak**
> **Us all get a soak.**

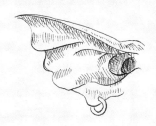

Typical ear of the average despot

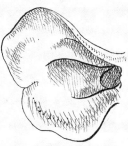

Good fighter or coward

11 Whereas some creatures make judgements about others according to the position of their eyes, it is useful to employ the same philosophy with regard to rats' ears.

Very bad fighter

Hairy ears, obviously mad

❦ APRIL ❦

12 On this day in 1665 the first victim of the plague to die in London was one Margaret Ponteous.

13 Frogs are particularly wary of the weather at this time of year, for they know full well that:

**An April flood do wash away
Ma Frog and her brood.**

14 The end of Alder month (squirrel calendar)

Three excellent dyes may be extracted from the Alder; green from its flowers, red from the bark and brown from the twigs, and so banners are made from these colours and set fluttering this night to herald in the next month.

❦ APRIL ❧

15

The beginning of Willow month (squirrel calendar)

After the enforced gloom of the previous months this is a carefree time when the old custom of making the briding basket is kept. Young squirrel maidens who wish to wed this year run to the Willow tree on this morning and beg of it some withys so that they may weave a small basket which will be carried upon their marriage day.

16

From the writings of the alchemist Dr Elias Theophrastus Spittle:

The Diamond, that most beautiful of stones, is joined with this month. A symbol of the male creative force in sorcery, the diamond would be a valued addition to the collection of magical apparatus I keep in the topmost room above the shop. Yet such trinkets must wait, for The Philosopher's Stone is the goal I must attain — above all else.

17

Now that the lowly nettle is flourishing, harvest the young tips with which to make delicious soup. Madame Akkikuyu used to cure her rheumatism by jumping into a clump of nettles and thrashing around until she was well and truly stung.

18

YELLOW

The hue of early flowers, it is a most heartening sight. The daffodil heralds the coming spring and so this is the colour of life and vitality. The buttery ochres of my pigments are always the ones I need to replace the most often, for my brush is ever generous where yellow is concerned.

19   Lost Sweethearts Day

The tragic mouse lovers of legend, Myrtle Cotton and Eglan Quince, perished upon this day when Eglan fell into the Thames and Myrtle leaped in to save him. Both were lost and their mournful tale is remembered in the dance 'Eglan and his Lady Love'. To see who their devoted sweethearts will prove to be, many mice fill a bowl with water this day and stare into it whilst brushing their hair. At the stroke of midnight the reflection of the one they will marry is supposed to appear in the water.

20   The Moon enters 'the Glutted Sack' (Rat Zodiac)

Also called 'Guzzlebag', 'Scoffpurse' and 'Gorger' this symbolises a rat's most basic craving, the lust for food. Many times during his life, a rat will fantasise of a paradise dripping with the juices of over-ripe and rancid delicacies. This blissful realm is symbolised by 'the Glutted Sack' where the drab realities of scrounging for left-overs and licking slime from drains are totally forgotten. The rat born at this time will always place the stuffing of his stomach and the satisfaction of his putrid taste buds above all else and so will prosper extremely well in sewer society.

Infamous Guzzlebags include: Kelly
Pigwiggen, the hedgehog

THE GLUTTED SACK

21

In the Willow month, to win the affection of the one you love, dig up a pawful of soil from their footprint on a morning when the moon is waxing and mix it with the earth about the roots of the Willow tree. As the tree grows, so will the heart of the one you desire become infatuated with you.

22

One of the fragments of sea lore gleaned from Thomas Triton is that a mouse with a noticeable blue vein upon his nose is doomed to die by drowning.

When he told me this, the midshipmouse became most disagreeable and took a great swig from his rum bowl before ordering me to get out. Upon leaving I could hear him calling out to his long lost friend and I felt woefully sorry for him in spite of his rudeness.

23

Taken from the Diary of Walter Thistlewick:

Today we of the Skirting's Morris and Sword Dancers, performed 'Hopping the Hare'. Well, as this is the easiest dance that we do, I thought it wud be a doddle. All the uther lads turn up reddy in there costyums, the hare hoods with the long ears sewed on and really lookd the part, exsept for that blessed Freddy Beechnut. He'd only gone and lost his proper hood and so made do with a cupple of twigs with a pair of mittens bunged on top. Put the mockers on the whole show that did. Then, to make matters werse when we did the 'hare boxing', Thickwit Freddy goes and knocks poor Percy Bobbin out cold.

24

The Herb Lore of Madame Akkikuyu:

Rosemary, she of savoury scent, flowers now. Where wife, she rule home and husband, it grow best. Mouseys bury dead with sprigs, to tell bucket kickers they not forget. Rosemary very good in lotions to make hair soft but strong, Akkikuyu must wash locks every April whether they dirty or not – her beauty too much to let slip.

APRIL

25

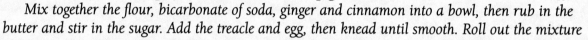

In the lead up to the Great Spring Festival, mice are now enjoying Blind Brass Biscuits. Gwen Triton has kindly allowed her recipe to be included in this almanack.

12oz flour	2 tsp bicarbonate of soda
2 tsp of ground ginger	4oz butter
6oz brown sugar	1 egg
4 tbsp of treacle	1 tsp ground cinnamon

Mix together the flour, bicarbonate of soda, ginger and cinnamon into a bowl, then rub in the butter and stir in the sugar. Add the treacle and egg, then knead until smooth. Roll out the mixture and cut out ring shapes with two different sized cups, then bake in a medium oven for about 10 minutes. When the brass biscuits are cool they are ready to eat.

Remember, only those youngsters who have not yet received a brass may partake of these, for with the first bite they are to wish for the sign that will see them throughout their adult lives.

26

In the year of Hobb's imprisonment within the acorn, the host of Moonriders were encamped about Hrethel's stronghold when a message came for Vesper to tell him of Ysabelle's inauguration as Starwife.

27

In Greenreach Vesper met Ysabelle to dissuade her from taking up the Starwifeship and to leave with him. Ysabelle refused and when Vesper was alone, the shade of Wendel Maculatum appeared to him. Regetting her decision, Ysabelle rushed back to tell Vesper but she was too late, the young bat was already dead and so she became the new Handmaiden of Orion – ruling for nearly three hundred years.

APRIL

28 With the Great Spring Ceremony so close, it is time to make new decorations for the Chambers of Summer and Winter.

29 On this night Madame Akkikuyu, the fortune-telling rat, visited the garden of the Deptford Mice to tell the fortunes of those daring enough to venture outside.

30 The day before the Great Spring Festival is a most exciting time for young mice. In the Skirtings this was when the Chambers of Winter and Summer were brought up from the cellar and dusted down for use in the next day's festivities.

Yet it is also a dangerous time when all manner of evils are let loose before the coming of Spring, when the Green is new born and it was upon this, unquiet night that Albert Brown was lured beyond the Grill and into the sewers where he was murdered by Jupiter.

MAY

❧ MAY ❦

1  This is the magical time of the Great Spring Festival when all mice celebrate the end of the cold months and look forward to the warmer days ahead. Upon this most holy day mousebrasses are given to those youngsters who have come of age and these shining amulets are treasured by them for the rest of their lives.
In the past, young Thomas Triton (Thomas Stubbs as he was called then) went in search of his friend Woodget Pipple from Betony Bank Farm upon this day and so began his seafaring life upon the Calliope. But perhaps the most marvellous event to be recorded at the time of the Great Spring Festival was the appearance of the Green Mouse himself to Audrey Brown to present her with a very special mousebrass from his own shimmering coat.

The Anti-Cat Charm

2 Sore heads are a common ailment today after drinking too much Berrybrew at the previous evening's festivities. A customary remedy is a hot mustard poultice applied to the back of a mouse's neck.
In the early hours of this morning, Audrey Brown slipped from The Skirtings to visit Madame Akkikuyu in the sewers where she also encountered the young city mouse, Piccadilly.

3 Twit was flown by Orfeo and Eldritch to Greenwich where he first met Thomas Triton on board the Cutty Sark. It was also the time when Audrey was captured by the rats and witnessed the fight between Fletch and One-eyed Jake in the pagan temple dedicated to the Raith Sidhe. In that horrible place, Fletch's blood was spilled upon the altar of Bauchan and so his slumbering spirit was awakened.

❧ MAY ❧

4 **A most joyous day and one now held high in the calendars of most creatures.** Before the dawn, Jupiter's earthly body was finally destroyed with the aid of Audrey's mousebrass and was drowned in the deep dark sewer water.

The traditional springtime tune "Old Mog's Drowning" has since become associated with this day and new steps were added to the jig by Algy Coltfoot to represent the evil Lord of the Rats' watery demise.

5  Returning from his adventures in the sewers, Oswald Chitter was put straight to bed with a severe chill which steadily grew worse as the days passed by.

A peeled onion is thought to attract the germs which cause infection and so is commonly found by the beds of sick mice.

A roasted onion kept pressed against the ear is very good for earache and the young mice believed it could help diminish the pain of Master Oldnose's cane if the juice was rubbed on to the palms of their paws.

6 Upon the 'Calliope' Woodget Pipple first met Dimlon (in truth Dahrem Ruhar - one of the adepts of the Scale).

7 Jupiter's drowned corpse was washed out of the sewers and into the River Thames.

✣ MAY ✣

8 Thomas and Woodget consulted the great prophet - Simoon, the jerboa - who told the midshipmouse's fortune.

The cards of Simoon which foretold Thomas' unhappy future

9 The shrine of Virbius in Crete where the Green Mouse is believed to have first sprung from the barren earth was destroyed by the evil forces of Scarophion, the Dark Despoiler. The storm which followed their ship caused the Calliope to be destroyed and if it were not for Zenna the sea maiden, Woodget would have perished in the churning waves.

10 The rotting body of Jupiter was cast from the river on to the shore at Deptford.

11 Jupiter's carcass was finally consumed in a bonfire but the black oily smoke which rose from the burning hung over the district for two days.

❦ MAY ❧

12

The last day of the Willow month (squirrel calendar)
All briding baskets should now be completed and put away until the day
of marriage. Ill luck and unhappiness shall follow those maidens who
have failed to complete the task unless they propitiate the tree from
which the willow was cut with five different flowers and tie them to its
topmost branches.

13

The beginning of the Hawthorn month (squirrel calendar)
A time to gather the heady blossom, to decorate the home
and to make delicious Hawthorn Blossom Cup.
The Hawthorn is the symbol of one of the five branches of the noble black
squirrels. Little is known about them as they were ever secretive and closed
their borders to outsiders many hundreds of years ago, never to be heard from again. But
their queen was said to be an enchantress who cast spells with a branch of Hawthorn
blossom and so is most powerful during this month.

*The golden badge of the
secret realm, worn at the
throat of the Queen.*

14

Master William Scuttle (Twit) was born on this day in Fennywolde to
Gladwin and Elijah. When he was young, he was considered to be a
simpleton by the other fieldmice. 'No cheese upstairs,' they would say.
He proved his worth however and gained their respect in that tragic summer when
Audrey and Arthur Brown arrived from Deptford with Madame Akkikuyu. William
Scuttle is now King of the Field but misses his friends and has vowed to return to
Deptford one day.

✦❦ MAY ❦✦

15 According to the legends of Coll Regalis (the Hazel Realm), the first sacred streams began to flow through the forest on this day and the spirit of the Green spread his power throughout the land.

16 🌙 The bats consider the Hawthorn month to be an unlucky time and will make no new prophecies until 'Uath's moon' is waning.

17

St Osfrid's monument

The fast day of Osfrid, the mouse martyr, whom legend proclaims was the first creature to be peeled in the name of Hobb.

    A sad time when it is advisable to recount the terrifying stories of the three rat gods (the Raith Sidhe) to the young so that they might remember the terrible threat the unholy triad pose.

18 Even now a frost is still possible so it is prudent to remember the old Fennywolde saying,

    Don't drag your tail about, till May is out.

❧ MAY ❧

19
The moon enters the sign of the Claw
(Rat Zodiac)

A rat born under this ferocious symbol, vulgarly called 'Gouger', is said to be one of the most savage and brutal of those loathsome creatures. Many rats contrive to have their offspring born at this time, but woe betide a matron who carries over into the shameful Mouse sign.

Infamous Gouger rats include: Smiler

Vinegar Pete

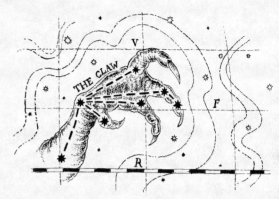

20
Beware brooms made in the month of May for they will sweep all luck out of the nest.

21
From the writings of the alchemist Dr Elias Theophrastus Spittle:

The gemstone associated with this month is the emerald. This prized jewel, also known as the Beryl, is dedicated to Venus and has influence over all matters of the heart. It is also said to possess the virtue of turning serpents' eyes to liquid should they look into its depths. (This last statement is completely false as I have proven at considerable hazard and jeopardy to mine own person!)

22 A good time for the young mice of The Skirtings to venture out into the garden to hunt for sticks to fight with. Arthur Brown still has two of his favourite 'ratbeaters' as he calls them.

23 The oaks of Greenwich Park are now in leaf and the Starwife likes to wander in their bright green shade.

24 One of the most annoying aspects of this time of year is the near constant racket from the blackbirds who refuse to keep quiet. One of them has been outside my window all day and I am finding it almost impossible to concentrate!

❧ MAY ❧

25

(squirrel sign language)
This is the oldest sign, meaning "shelter" or "home", safety and protection.

26 Two years after moving to Holeborn and becoming the new Thane, Arthur Brown married Nel Poot. Many of the mice from the 'Cutty Sark' made the journey to celebrate the wedding. Gwen Triton, however, attended the event alone as Thomas was too 'ill' to travel and his sister, the Starwife, was too busy with her high office.

27 Depending on the weather (or marauding owls), the Hall of Corn is constructed in Fennywolde about this time.

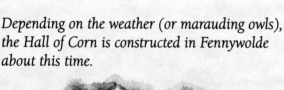

28 Upon this night Audrey Scuttle finally ascended the observatory hill in Greenwich and beneath the twinkling heavens became the new Starwife.

❧ MAY ❧

29 At sunrise, gather up a pawful of dew and wash your whiskers with it. This is a potent charm and the first likely fellow you meet will love you evermore. No doubt Alison Sedge, the fieldmouse, performed this ritual as many times as possible to make Jenkin Nettle jealous.

30 Larder raids common about now.

One of the gruesome masks worn at the feast of "Goregut"

31  *The dreaded rat feast of Goregut.*
A vile and debauched day of slaughter and wickedness when it is wisest to remain indoors. Held in honour of the Raith Sidhe, this pagan custom nearly died out in Deptford during Jupiter's time and was remembered only by the likes of One-eyed Jake and his crew. But elsewhere the horrible festival lives on and many a mouse has wandered too far from home, never to return, when 'the peelers are a hunting'.
Best advice for this day is - keep the door bolted and stay in bed!

JUNE

JUNE

1 On this morning the now unhinged Madame Akkikuyu was captured in Greenwich Park by many frightened grey squirrels and brought before the old Starwife.

2 **From the writings of the alchemist Dr Elias Theophrastus Spittle:**

The stone linked to this uncomfortable and sweltering month is the Agate, which endows the wearer with health and has the virtue of healing fevers. For this reason alone I have been spared the ravages of the Smallpox and the Meezles. The very notion of disease and administering to the infected frights me most brutally, is it not a cruel irony which cast me in the role of apothecary?

3 In 1665 Will heard the distant thundering of the battle between the English and Dutch navies echoing up the River Thames.

༄ JUNE ༄

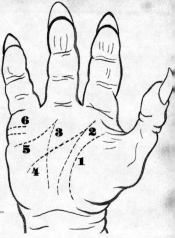

4  With only a little time left of the savage 'Gouger' star sign, now is an excellent time for the reading of palms. Madame Akkikuyu was a supreme mistress of this art and could tell a great deal merely by looking at another rat's claw.

1 Murder line - ruled by Hobb
2 Luck line - ruled by Mabb
3 Health line
4 Cunning line - ruled by Bauchan
5 Courage line
6 Enemies to be overcome

---

5 This is the season for the elderflower to bloom. It is a most wonderful ingredient in the fermenting of the finest wines, as Tom Cockle was always eager to point out. I wonder what it is about the name Tom that makes every one I encounter too fond of the bottle?

6 **The moon leaves the house of Hobb and enters the sign of The Mouse (Rat Zodiac)**

Although the time of The Mouse endures for only nine days it is an extremely ill omen for a ratwife to bear rat offspring in this period. Known by many base, scornful titles, 'Runt time', 'Sickweed', 'Milkmites', 'Gnatbrat' and 'Shrimpspawner' to name but few, a ratling born now is seen to be weak and cowardly, never rises in the ranks and is always spat upon.

A ratwife will induce labour before 'The Claw' sign is ended or strive to hold onto the unborn child until The Mouse is over. Yet many have also murdered their 'Sickweed' young, rather than endure the stigma of being a 'Milkmite' mother.

Because of the disgrace that this time bestows, there are no infamous rats recorded here.

---

7 On this day Thomas Triton took Audrey Brown and Twit to see the Starwife in Greenwich. Consequently Oswald Chitter was snatched from the brink of death by the magic of the Starwife, but the price of this miraculous cure was that Audrey had to journey to Fennywolde with Madame Akkikuyu.

JUNE

8 Hearing that Audrey was to leave the Skirtings, but misunderstanding the reason, Piccadilly slipped sadly away in the early hours of this morning and began the long trek back to the City.

9  **The last day of the Hawthorn month (squirrel calendar)**
Now are the bats finally released from the unlucky influence of Uath's moon and free to make new prophecies.

10  **The Oak Month begins (squirrel calendar)**
The Oak is the most revered of all trees. It is well known that the first squirrel awoke in its branches in the deeps of time and found the silver acorn which became the talisman of the Starwives, hanging there. In the past, to celebrate and honour this noble season, the monarchs of each royal house would light an Oak fire and there would be great feasting and merrymaking. But since the fall of the ancient kingdoms this custom is remembered only by the making of Oak leaf crowns which are often worn upon this night by the squirrels of Greenwich.

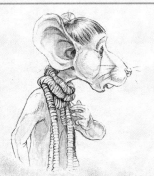

11 A year after his friends Arthur and Audrey, Oswald Chitter was born on this day to Arabel and Jacob and although no one pays any attention to the ridiculous claims of the Rat Zodiac, Master Oswald was very frail and sickly. During the terrible year when Jupiter was deposed however, the albino mouse proved his worth many times, culminating in his tragic loss upon the observatory hill when he plunged into the void. Having never reached his 'coming of age' Oswald Chitter was posthumously awarded the mousebrass signifying courage and bravery by the Green Mouse himself.

12  ***The Herb Lore of Madame Akkikuyu:***

'Valerian, she flowering now. Very good, very useful in potions to calm and peace any mad flapper. Akkikuyu like smelly pong of Valerian root – she had jar of root squeezies and like to rub ears with the juice. But big kittys like whiff too, so Akkikuyu no wear it now – she chased too many times.'

---

13 On their journey to Fennywolde, Twit and Arthur learned many of Kempe's disreputable songs, including the trader's favourite:

> *Poor Rosie! Poor Rosie!*
> *I'll tell you of poor Rosie,*
> *The tragedy that was Rosie*
> *And why she died so lonely;*
>
> *Coz for all her looks her armpits stank,*
> *The suitors came, but away they shrank*
> *Far away from Rosie,*
> *With their paws tight on their nosey.*

---

14 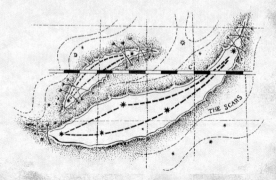 ***After the humiliating time of 'The Mouse', the Rat Zodiac moves into the house of Mabb and the moon enters the sign of 'The Scars' also known as 'Big Bleeder' and 'Little Bleeder'.***

To have a birthday in 'The Scars' is most honourable. Representing every injury gained in battle, this sign denotes a warrior who will not shrink from his duty and will fight to the last claw and fang.

During this time, if it rains on a night when there is no moon, it is said to be The Scars' blood which pours and to drink of 'the weeping wounds' kindles and heightens a rat's hideous bloodlust.

Infamous Bleeders include: *Vinny*
Smiff

15 Now the days are long and hot. It is an excellent time to gather herbs and dry them in the sun. Mice are particularly fond of making herbal wreaths, not only are they decorative but it is also a practical way of storing them for culinary purposes.

16 On this day in 1665 the mother of Jupiter, Imelza, was killed by frightened Londoners who thought that the cats and dogs of the city were spreading the plague.

17  **VIRIDIAN**
In the month when the spirit of the Green is most powerful, what other shade could be so appropriate? The colour of growth and nature, it has an harmonious lushness and to see the hillocks of Greenwich carpeted with emerald is a spectacle which even I fail to capture.

18 This was the day when the Chandi arrived in the city of Hara and the young Thomas Triton and his friend Woodget were taken to the Sadhu.

JUNE

19 In the early hours, the forces of Sarpedon assailed the gates of Hara and swarmed within weilding venom tipped blades. The battle that followed was bloody and cruel, and many innocent citizens perished in the terrible violence.

20 The country mouse keeps his eyes peeled during this month as he goes about his business, for the Green Mouse is supposed to visit and bless the hedgerows and to spy Him bodes wondrous joy and fortune.

21 It was on this day that Audrey, Arthur, and Madame Akkikuyu first arrived in Fennywolde and the fortune-teller drove away Mahoot the owl, to the delight of the fieldmice.

JUNE

22 This was when Audrey made the corn dolly which was to wreak such havoc and terror to the Fennywolders. For, upon this night, Madame Akkikuyu hearkened to the tattoo on her ear and by its arts brought the straw effigy to life.

23 The magical Midsummer's Eve when the Green Mouse is at his most powerful. It is the time when all creatures are safe from harm, for all evil things are powerless. In a Hawthorn grotto, illuminated by a wondrous light emanating from the leaves, The Green Mouse appeared to the Fennywolders this night – but the following day only Audrey remembered.

24 This night Madame Akkikuyu, guided by Nicodemus, cast a spell to make it rain but in the early morning, Young Whortle was murdered in the mist by the animated corn dolly.

JUNE

25 In spite of Madame Akkikuyu's efforts to save him, Jenkin Nettle was killed by Mahoot the owl.

26 To save Audrey Brown from being hanged, William Scuttle invoked the Fennywolde gallows law and married her this night. Later, Nicodemus revealed himself to be Jupiter's unquiet spirit returned from the eternal void and upon learning this, Madame Akkikuyu sacrificed herself to the flames which destroyed the Hall of Corn.

27

A good time for beetles

Madame Akkikuyu always kept her eyes open for these insects, for they were a staple ingredient of her cures and potions. To keep one trapped inside a hazelnut shell was a sure antidote for a cough.

Thomas Triton however, disagrees and says that the old mariners swore that to kill a black beetle would bring seven days of rain.

Personally I hate the horrid insects, for they get into my pigments then scamper across my paintings — ruining them and leaving peculiar streaks and marks behind. I have squished three already this week and so far there has been not one drop of rain, so there you are Mister Triton!

28  The Anti-Owl charm. There were many of these worn in Fennywolde during the time of Mahoot's reign and not one of the bearers were ever snatched by his talons.

JUNE

29 ***Delicious strawberries are now plentiful***
    Rats are always guzzling this fruit and have been known to devour an entire field-full. These nuisances can be driven away with sticks, but be careful not to eat too many strawberries – for swollen stomachs make weary work for the legs should the rats return desiring a more savoury mouthful.

30 Thomas and Woodget arrived in Singapore on this day, having escaped from the fallen city of Hara and drank at the Lotus Parlour where a young Madame Akkikuyu first took up the profession of fortune-teller after stealing some of Simoon the prophet's magical paraphernalia.

JULY

1 Within the Black Temple of Suruth Scarophion, the dreaded serpent's foul hopes of return were finally dashed due to the hallowing of the ninth segment of the eggshell.

2 Finally the arduous clean-up operations after the fire in Fennywolde were completed and the fieldmice were at last able to mourn for their lost King of the Field and the others who had perished.

3 On this day Madame Akkikuyu was buried by the still pool at Fennywolde. Ever afterwards that spot was said to be a magical place where wishes were granted, especially to young mouse maidens on warm summer evenings, when the setting sun shone upon the grass under which the fortune-teller lay.

❧ JULY ❧

4 **The blackest day of Thomas Triton's life**
The time he was compelled to drown his friend Woodget Pipple by the evil art of Mother Lotus.

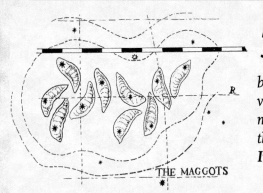

THE MAGGOTS

5 **The moon enters the sign of The Maggots (Rat Zodiac)**
Mabb is the dark Lady of Midnight Slaughter, yet also the bringer of pestilence as this constellation reminds us. A rat born at this time will be corrupt and rotten right through, with no redeeming virtue. He is a loner who shifts his allegiance to whoever is in power and must never be trusted. Yet this faithless quality is considered to be a worthwhile trait in this barbaric society and many rats are proud to be ruled by this particular sign.
Infamous Maggot Rats include: Morgan
Fletch

6 In 1653 Master William Godwin was born to Sarah and Daniel in the Oxfordshire village of Adcombe. Destined to become the apprentice of Doctor Elias Theophrastus Spittle, he eventually returned to Adcombe and took over his father's lands which had been stolen from him and died peacefully in his sleep at the ripe age of eighty-nine.

7 **The end of the Oak month (squirrel calendar)**
Taken from the Diary of Walter Thistlewick:

As usual we of the Skirting's Morris and Sword Dancers, performed 'Caper the Betty' today. What a shambols! Thick hedded Freddy Beechnut refused to wear the raggy dress and be the Betty, coz he sedd it was Sissy. So us poor lot had to 'Caper the Berty' instedd. I just hope Herbert Chickweed's leg gets better soon so we can put a stop to this nonsenss.

8  **_The beginning of Holly month (squirrel calendar)_**
If the Oak is the king of trees then surely the Holly is the prince. In days of old the squirrel houses actually selected eight Holly Princes from their ranks upon this day to officiate over the lesser ceremonies and be ambassadors to other realms.

9 _Finally I have managed to draw the Great Oak. Legend tells that this is the very one grown from the acorn which imprisoned the pagan rat god, Hobb, by Ysabelle the Starwife, in the dim and distant past._
The tree has been dead for many centuries but still a part of it stands, supported by a mighty growth of ivy about the trunk and while a splinter of it remains it is said that the Lord of the Raith Sidhe can never return.

10 The day that Audrey and Arthur left Fennywolde
- never to return.

JULY

11  *From the writings of the alchemist Dr Elias Theophrastus Spittle:*

The Ruby is a most useful gemstone. Linked with this month, these precious drops of gore signify courage just like the Bloodstone. For the summoning of spirits 'tis always prudent to wear a Ruby, for they do help control it, whether its nature be good or ill. How well I doth like this jewel, for it reminds me of the flowing auburn hair which was mine in the days of youth — oh how the recollection brings on the melancholy and my tears besmudge the page.

12  *At last the day dawned which I have long been dreading. That bothersome hedgehog, Pirkin Gim-Gim, finally kept his promise and came to visit. I had to keep a constant vigil to stop him from tinkering with my pots of pigment. There was only one thing worth hearing in the whole of his visit — the sighting of two rats come lately to Greenwich. As this place has been deserted by the creatures since the fall of Jupiter, except for Dodder, my informant, I found this curious and told the Starwife at once.*

13 During this broiling heat it is advisable to look for a stone or pebble in which a hole has been worn through the centre. This is a sure protection against adders which are numerous at this time of year.

14  **Baffles Day**
This is when you should keep a watch on small trinkets. Now, more than any other season, they are disposed to disappear and lose themselves.
On the return home from Fennywolde, Audrey mislaid one of her tail bells upon this day.

JULY

15 The Herb Lore of Madame Akkikuyu:
'Wild Thyme, she a-flowering. Oh, many stories about this herb
– yes, yes, yes. The perfume – it belongs to
dead. Where jab-jabbing murder happen, that place
be always haunted by thyme scent. Akkikuyu,
she use it when tooth fangs ache, crushed
leaves rubbed on soreness make pain go.'

16 During this time of haymaking, the country creatures must look
to their homes and be ready to run from both scythe and mower.

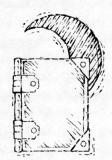

17 ***The Black Night of Hrethel***
In the distant past, the most infamous of all bats ascended to become Keeper
of the Great Book and was enslaved to it by his greed and lust for power. It was
he who started the first of the holy wars with the squirrels. All bats are silent this night and curse
Hrethel in their hearts.

18 Today Fitz told me in his usual simpering and superior manner, that the
Starwife wishes me to go to Fennywolde to interview the folk there, as it
would undoubtedly aid me in my work. It will be a long journey and I
have already begun to pack.

19   *The Sign of Life*

This mousebrass, along with the Sign of Hope, is normally bestowed upon those whose struggles in life will be difficult and demanding, with little or no reward. This brass is given to them as a reminder that their endeavours are never in vain and to inspire them to overcome the obstacles placed in their path. Jenkin Nettle bore this sign and it was this which his father discovered in the owl pellet of Mahoot after his son was murdered

The Sign of Life

20

In this roasting weather be sure to protect your ears, nose and tail from burning.

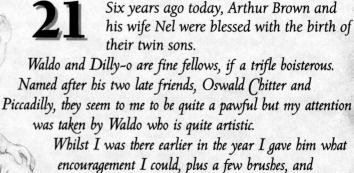

21

Six years ago today, Arthur Brown and his wife Nel were blessed with the birth of their twin sons.

Waldo and Dilly-o are fine fellows, if a trifle boisterous. Named after his two late friends, Oswald Chitter and Piccadilly, they seem to me to be quite a pawful but my attention was taken by Waldo who is quite artistic.

Whilst I was there earlier in the year I gave him what encouragement I could, plus a few brushes, and although it will be a long time before he could compete with a professional such as me, he has a pleasing, if homely, little talent.

22

If the dry weather is proving unbearable, make a note of the next drop of rain and see the direction it comes from for, according to Old Todmore:

Rain from the South'll stop the drought
From the North only dust'll spring forth
A splash out the East'll soak any beast
But a shower from the West be always best.

Rum swilling buffoon!

23

To raise a favourable wind whilst at sea
Thomas Triton relates that the old mariners would cast a pawful of gull feathers or thistledown into the air and blow it in the direction they wished the wind to gust.

I could not help but laugh at this dollop of foolishness, upon which the old sot snapped that I was merely the one making the almanack — whereas it was the Green who made the weather. How I dislike his crusty bad manners. I have a good mind to scribble over the drawings I have made of him and write something very rude beneath them!

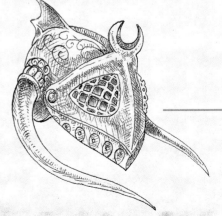

24 ☾

The great hero, Rohgar's screechmask - 'slaughtermaw'.

JULY

25  **AZURE**
I have always adored the fierce blue skies of this month and so this delicious colour sits here. It is the hue of tranquility and it is said that spirits appear in a blue light – and though I have no personal evidence of this the Starwife has confirmed it.

26 The constellation of Gorscarrigern which appears in the heavens when the serpent's spirit draws near to the living plane.

> Nine bright stars from out the void
> shining up on high
> whose banished soul do they call back
> and augur in the sky?
> Despoiler of the ancient lands,
> who baked the deserts dry.
> Scarophion, Scarophion – the demon is close by.

27 That wretched Pirkin Gim-Gim has been doodling upon my finest parchment. Just wait until the next time I see him!

28 During the diseased sign of the Maggots, Madame Akkikuyu would cure warts with this simple but unfair charm.
'Count how many wartylumps you have, then find as many tiny, baby stones and wrap in ivy leaf. Go quick-trip to roadside, dig deep to bury and run. On the nose of first passer by, the wartylumps will appear and you be free. Now, you no go play with toadies no more.'

JULY

29 To seal the bond between two sweethearts, red squirrels would often cut their initials from a piece of paper and stick them to an apple when it was still growing upon the tree. In the coming weeks their love would ripen with the fruit and in the autumn, when the apple was red, the paper would be removed and the initials found to be still green. Then would the couple share the fruit to complete the charm.

I recall that I tried this when I was young with a pretty maid called Tormentil — alas when we bit into our apple we discovered that it was full of worms and so we parted.

30 Sudden thunderstorms are to be expected now but take great care where you shelter, many fieldmice have darted into the nearest hole only to be met by a row of sharp teeth and quickly devoured. The current wisdom is to quell the instinctive urge to head for cover and instead hurry home as quickly as possible.

31  ***Extract from the travelling journal of Gervase Brightkin – Day 13***

Today I arrived in Fennywolde and was met with great friendliness by Master William Scuttle, the present King of the Field. I must admit it is a most pleasant place and the nests are much more comfortable than I had imagined. Yet, hardly had I set my pack down when a crowd of excited fieldmice started plying me with questions about the doings of their friends in Greenwich and the City. Fortunately Mr Scuttle (I feel I cannot call him Twit) rescued me from their curiosity and it was wonderful to note the great respect which the others have for him.

AUGUST

AUGUST

1 The Night of Harvested Souls

An uncanny time of year, when those creatures who have died by the action of the harvester are said to return to walk again within the corn fields. On this night the youngsters of Fennywolde like to frighten themselves by telling ghost stories and snuggle up inside their nests, listening for the spectres of those who have 'gone ahead', to tread the ground beneath.

2 This evening, in Fennywolde I showed William Scuttle some of the drawings I have made of his friends. He was most keen to see Thomas Triton and Arthur Brown after all these years and chattered unceasingly about the times they had together. Yet when I showed to him the picture of the Starwife upon the Living Throne he fell silent. It was clear to me that he misses her most of all, for though they were wed to save her from the noose, it is plain he truly loves her.

3 Thomas Triton always tells the younger mice never to turn their mattresses over on a Friday as to do this will turn ships at sea.

For myself, I think he would do well to curb his drinking. Why — some of the gibberish he spouts is downright ludicrous! Still, I am reminded of the old proverb, 'he that is weatherwise is not otherwise'.

⋙ AUGUST ⋘

4 *The end of the Holly month (squirrel calendar)*

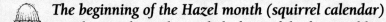

5 *The beginning of the Hazel month (squirrel calendar)*
The Hazel was the symbol of one of the five royal houses of black squirrels. Second in importance to Greenreach, Coll Regalis, the Hazel Realm was ruled by wisdom alone – for no magic guarded its borders, only the vigilance of the sentries and squirrel archers kept the enemies at bay (unless the enchanted Hazelnut could be found at the time of Wisdom Gathering). Coll Regalis was eventually destroyed by the fire eggs of the Moonriders when the Lady Ninnia was queen, many hundreds of years ago.

6 In Fennywolde many ancient customs are kept alive, such as the belief that a bowl kept in the boughs of an oak would be filled with blessed water straight from the Green.

7 *Now is the time for all swallows to be fearful.*
It is said that these birds keep a magical stone in their bodies which, if removed during the August full moon, has the power to cure blindness and if placed under the tongue will make it eloquent.

❧ AUGUST ☙

8   *Extract from the travelling journal of Gervase Brightkin – Day 21*

Today I left Fennywolde. It was a most merry departure and I was in high spirits until a figure stepped suddenly from the hedge by my side.

The creature had a dishevelled appearance but I guessed the identity. Alison Sedge is a country beauty no more, she looks more like a rat, and even then the scruffiest of them all. Some say that she is now a witch, but the poor soul is obviously crazed. And yet I am not sure... fixing me with a ghastly stare which caused every hair upon my tail to stand on end she pointed up the path and in a solemn, croaking voice gave me this very warning.

'Ten years has the one who robbed my Love sat upon the Living Throne, but soon her reign will end and she will know more loss than poor mad Alison.'

With that she leaped back into the hedgerow, but I have to confess that I was rather shaken and wonder if I should relate the incident to the Starwife.

9   *From the writings of the alchemist Dr Elias Theophrastus Spittle:*

The stone of this month is the Sardonyx. A gem of very little note, this has the dubious property of ensuring contentment and happiness in the wretched and foolhardy state of matrimony. The other more interesting virtue it is supposed to hold is the ability to allow the bearer to walk invisibly amongst others. This is of course absurd yet would it not be a delight to walk unseen and dine at the highest tables on spice cakes and syllabubs rather than the usual hodgepodge I am obliged to serve mineself.

10   In the late summer it is the custom amongst many fieldmice maidens to wear a buttercup in their hair 'for the sun's sake'. It is said that this will bring the Daystar cheer as its strength begins to falter and fail.

AUGUST

11 — Tysle Day

This is the time when the brave little shrew was found amongst hundreds of bodies after a Hobber attack, by Giraldus the mole. Tysle is the Shrews' greatest hero and they honour his memory upon this day by acting out 'Hobble Plays' which are the highlight of the shrew year. To be picked for the lead in such performances is a great honour and commands much esteem afterwards. For the rest of the community there are always the Mole Strings which are an essential part of the festivities, and no self respecting shrew would be seen without one of them tied about his or her waist this day.

12 — The Herb Lore of Madame Akkikuyu:

'Flowers of Wood Sage now been open long time. This herb, he very good for the gum scurvy. Akkikuyu be mighty unhappy if tooth fangs fall out, so she pick leaves and brew to make a sippy tea. Round and round she swills then spit gobby out. Akkikuyu do this till the scurvy it better and her she have old ravishy smile back.'

13

Wild poppies are now blooming in the cornfields, but the country folk are careful not to pick them, for to do so is sure to bring a storm, hence the poppy's Fennywolde name – 'Thundercup'.

14

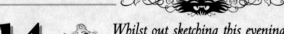

Whilst out sketching this evening, I had the misfortune to encounter the two rats Pirkin Gim-Gim spoke of. They are not young, one of them was bald with a most sour looking face, whilst the other is the owner of a dreadful squint. Although they were neither rude nor threatened me, I began to grow exceedingly nervous and when I asked their names they sniggered most hideously. Mercifully, a group of sentries chose that moment to call out from the boughs overhead and the two rats left quickly. Still, it has shaken me and I have done no more work tonight as my paws won't stop trembling. I must tell the Starwife this news at once.

AUGUST

15  Today the Starwife has despatched her sentries to look for the two rats I met yesterday and bring them before her. But what a job she had with those jittery grey cousins of mine. They refused to depart in groups of less than fifteen.

16 *From the writings of the alchemist Dr Elias Theophrastus Spittle: 1665*

'Tis the feast day of Saint Roch, the plague doctor who lived three centuries since. His name have I invoked to protect me from all pestilence. I pray that the charm be true, with every other house shut up and painted with the red cross, the very air is foetid with a foul miasma of death and disease — and I quail in my undergarments.

17 **Rooting Festival**
The night when all moles gather and hold great revel in their underground chambers. No other creature has ever witnessed this event, for moles guard their secrets well. However, many accounts tell of the strange music which can be heard echoing from beneath the ground on this night.

18 **The moon enters the sign of the 'Ratwitch' (Rat Zodiac)**
Also known as 'Haggers', 'Cronies' and 'Madame Hex', the rat born now will be drawn towards all things mystical and will most probably join the ranks of the countless charlatans and hoodwinking fortune-tellers. Usually these Ratwitches are harmless, a factor which makes them more approachable than the rest of ratkind and so normally timid creatures will feel less afraid of seeking their advice.
Infamous Ratwitches include: Ma Skillet
Although not a rat, the squirrel arch-traitor Morwenna was born at this time.

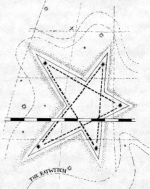

THE RATWITCH

---

19 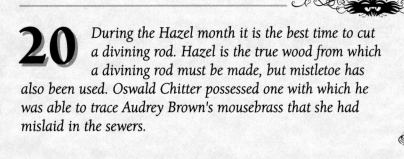 At last the two itinerant rats were discovered skulking in a deserted rabbit hole and were brought before the Starwife.

The rats are none other than *Vinegar Pete* and *Leering Macky* who were believed to have perished with the rest of *Jupiter's* crew more than ten years ago!

The Starwife was visibly jolted on seeing them, and for some moments was unable to speak. Eventually she commanded the rats to leave this land at once. Yet, when they departed, the ugly pair were heard to chuckle to themselves most insolently.

Now Fitz has declared that no one is safe, for they are rats of *Jupiter* and as such, filled with the blood lust he set into them.

20 During the Hazel month it is the best time to cut a divining rod. Hazel is the true wood from which a divining rod must be made, but mistletoe has also been used. Oswald Chitter possessed one with which he was able to trace Audrey Brown's mousebrass that she had mislaid in the sewers.

---

21 When the moon is waning in this month, gather up the seeds of flowers you wish to plant the following year and store them in a dry place.

22

A map of that land
known as Fennywolde.

A *The field where the hall of corn is made*
B *The fieldmice's winter quarters*
C *The meadow*
D *The oaks where Mahoot the owl dwelt*
E *The ditch where the corn dolly was given life*
F *The still pool*
G *Madame Akkikuyu's burial place*
H *Mr Woodruffe's mound*

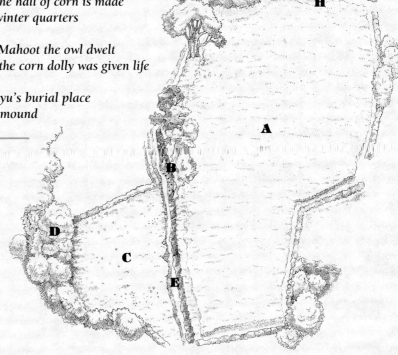

23

In 1665 at the height of the plague,
apothecaries sold London Treacle – a
foul mixture to ward off the pestilence,
made from oil, gunpowder and sacke.

24

During the month of the Ratwitch, I have copied out a magic box
so popular amongst the ratfolk, who wear them rolled up in pouches
about their filthy necks to ward off the curses of their enemies.

25  ***The Herb Lore of Madame Akkikuyu:***
Rue plant, it very good to keep adder poison away. Akkikuyu always keep in bag, if she meet slithery snake she have big chew to save her if he bite. Rue also good for curses, throw it at victim and shout, 'You mean old snotsucker – you will rue this day!', then hit him hard with bag just to make sure.

26 **Harebells now in bloom**
These flowers of the harvest are protected by the influence of the Lady of the Moon and so to pick them is most unlucky.

27 Beware of staggering rats at this time, for they are undoubtedly afflicted with sunstroke, having neglected to don their rat hoods. In their blistering pain, they are driven to all kinds of violence and create much mayhem.

 **28**  **The Sign of Hate**
This accursed mousebrass was made by Isaac Nettle in his wrath for Audrey Brown, whom he blamed for the death of his son, Jenkin. This was an important element in releasing Jupiter's spirit upon the world.

AUGUST

29 The harvest is well under way now and the Fennywolders are forced to return to their winter quarters when their Hall of Corn is destroyed.

30 (squirrel sign language)
To see this carved into the bark of a tree or even scratched into the ground strikes fear into the heart of any squirrel. It is a signal telling all to beware, there is great danger close by and it would be best to seek shelter at once or turn back completely and return home.

31 Except for Fennywolde, the custom of making corn dollies is popular now amongst country mice, for they provide a place for the spirit of the crop to harbour and sit out the winter until the following spring.

SEPTEMBER

❧ SEPTEMBER ❧

1 🌰 The end of the Hazel month (squirrel calendar)

Seen as a time when wisdom fails, this is the day when dunces and idiots are forgiven their lack of wits and even learned scholars are permitted to indulge in tomfoolery.

2 🌰 The beginning of the Vine month (squirrel calendar)

For the black squirrels, the Vine symbolised the family and so the lineage of a royal household was always depicted about its leaves and branches.

This is also the day when the Great Fire of London began in 1666, and the time Leech drank of both the elixir of life and the orange hair colorant.

3

In 1666 Doctor Elias Theophrastus Spittle perished in flames when the reborn Magnus Zachaire dragged him into the fire. It was also the day when the real Jupiter died, betrayed by his envious brother Leech.

SEPTEMBER

4 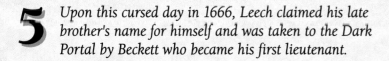 **Queen of the Harvest**
When all the corn is gathered in, fieldmice elect one of their maidens to be Queen of the Harvest. Wearing a crown of woven wheat ears, she takes over from the King of the Field and must officiate at all ceremonies and functions until the next Hall of Corn is made. In recent years, Pansy Clover, Daisy Bottom and Wormy Medlar have had the honour of wearing the crown.

5 Upon this cursed day in 1666, Leech claimed his late brother's name for himself and was taken to the Dark Portal by Beckett who became his first lieutenant.

6 About this time when moths are numerous, much fine sport is to be had for the bat weanings. They improve their agility and expertise in flight by pursuing these beautiful winged insects but, although young bats are partial to these beautiful insects, they will not always eat those that they catch. When he eventually becomes a Knight of the Moon a bat must adorn his wings with traditional motifs. But the lustrous pigment used is derived from the wing scrapings of certain moths, so when they indulge in these nightly chases, weanings will always carry a small jar with them to collect this shimmering yield.

7 (squirrel sign language)
This is the symbol of dearth and hunger, although its meaning has altered slightly during the passing of the ages. Mischievous youngsters, especially of the red squirrel houses, will often leave these outside the home of those they consider to be miserly or mean-spirited. To be pelted with empty acorn cups is an enormous insult and even the cheekiest youngster would never dream of doing that to anyone.

SEPTEMBER

8 The time when the webs of very large spiders are noticeable outdoors.
Rats will always bind a knife wound with cobwebs as they believe it will heal the quicker for it. I need hardly add that they will also eat the spider.

9 A rhyme often quoted by cats to their kittens:

> Prowl on a Monday, you'll kill by morning
> Hackles on a Tuesday, they rise for warning
> Purr on a Wednesday, you'll kiss a stranger
> Fight on a Thursday to get out of danger
> Lament on a Friday, you'll weep in sorrow
> Flee on a Saturday, spare time you'll borrow
> Stumble on a Sunday, your safety seek, for The Hunter will have you the rest of the week.

10 With apples ripening upon the trees, a squirrel takes extra care to ensure there are no late blossoms – as this portends certain death for someone dear.

11 The symbol of Family, three tails together, a most respectable and popular brass. Albert Brown possessed one, as did his son Arthur.

SEPTEMBER

12 — Barring the Master

This unusual ceremony seems to occur only in those places that have had contact with the mice of the Skirtings. On the morning of this day, the youngsters will barricade themselves in the place where they are given lessons and deny the tutor entry until he promises to give them a holiday.

I can only surmise that this was either an invention of Master Oldnose so that he might get on with mousebrass matters or the memory of a genuine revolt amongst his pupils. I wonder, were his lessons so tedious?

13 — From the writings of the alchemist Dr Elias Theophrastus Spittle:

Now the Sapphire makes this month its own. A gem of celestial beauty it is the symbol of feminine power and is imbued with much magical force. Known to dispel melancholia I have always held this stone in great esteem and keep a small jewel by me at all times. Thus do I stave off the shades of gloom, not only by its very presence but also by the memory of whence I came by it. 'Twas Sir Francis Lingley, that overblown, flouting popinjay from whom my small Sapphire was purloined. How I despise that man, may his liver and lights rot with the tinctures I shall prepare for him.

14 — Wisdom Gathering

The customary day for harvesting hazel nuts, the symbol of wisdom. In Coll Regalis this was a solemn time, for the fruit was highly regarded and it was widely known that there was always one special, magical hazelnut hidden amongst the rest, which would bestow three years of peace and protection on the realm if found before the setting of the sun. In the history scrolls of the Starwife it states quite clearly that only seven of these were ever found throughout the ages.

SEPTEMBER

15

The moon enters the sign of the 'Wheel' (Rat Zodiac)

Also called, 'Chancers', 'Jammybeggars', 'Flukers', 'Mabb-sends' and 'Ratty-go-lucky' this signifies the Wheel of Providence and Destiny. A rat born now is considered to be particularly lucky and will have a charmed existence throughout his life, escaping many dangers which, for others, would prove fatal.

Infamous Jammybeggars include: *Beckett*
Leering Macky

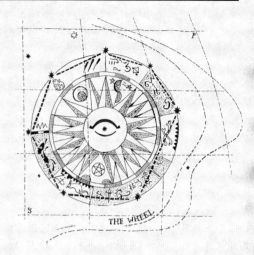

THE WHEEL

16

The Night of Nachteg

The barren ploughed fields of the countryside are the haunt of many dangerous spirits throughout the cold months, but one of the most perilous is Nachteg. Also known as the Midnight Death Hag, she roams the empty fields searching for victims from whom she sucks their blood. To prevent her crossing the threshold this night, country mice strew rose stems before their doorways in the belief that she will prick her feet upon the thorns and be too preoccupied in drinking her own blood to bother anyone else. Strange as this may sound, a number of the Fennywolders swear by the Green that they have discovered the stems scattered the next morning and dark red spots sprinkled upon the earth.

17

One of Kempe, the pedlar's, favourite songs at this time of year was:

When leaves do fall and the sun goes shy
I reach for my bowl and the hours roll by
For the juice of the berry do make me so merry
With my legs in the air, my head 'neath a chair,
I'll burp till the spring comes round again.

SEPTEMBER

18 Bawming the Yew

As the Oak is the King of the Wood and the Holly the prince, the Yew is surely the queen – but a dark and sinister one at that. The Yew tree is the tree of death. This is the morning when the grey squirrels link paws and circle the mightiest Yew of the district and ask of it to spare them, whilst tying green ribbons about its lowest branches. Many believe that 'Idho' the indwelling spirit, governs the precise time of their death and can be placated by this foolish ceremony. Most folk are still convinced that every root of a Yew tree seeks out the mouth of a buried corpse for nourishment.

19  During the sign of the Wheel, all worshippers of Hobb are wont to gamble and will congregate in their darksome holes to play with dice carved from the knuckle bones of some poor victim, draw lots, or roll plucked eyes in a macabre parody of marbles.

20 In 1666 Will and Molly returned to Adcombe, having escaped the terrors of the Great Fire.

21 The Night of the Elders

The time when the four leaders of the bat council are honoured.

Plan of a typical rat die

1 Go catch a mouse
2 Jump into the sewer water
3 Singe your whiskers
4 Snatch the other player's swag
5 Forfeit a fang
6 Eat the other player

SEPTEMBER

22

Rats are especially superstitious and most of them will always carry at least one lucky charm with them. Should a rat approach you in this season – take care! They believe that one of the most effective talismans is a mouse's little toe. Other 'fortune bringers' as they are called include hedgehog teeth and toad skins, both of which must be removed whilst the creature is still croaking or squealing on a moonless night.

23 The birthday of Thomas Triton

Originally called Thomas Stubbs, the seafaring mouse adopted the name Triton in memory of his best friend, Woodget Pipple, who often teased him with it after their encounter with the water maidens. After many years as a mariner, the midshipmouse eventually settled in Greenwich where the old Starwife eased his unhappy heart. Thomas Triton now lives on board the Cutty Sark, inside a hollow figurehead, with his wife Gwen.

24

Blackberries are now ripe in the hedgrows. It is the perfect time for picking and enjoying this wonderful and favourite fruit of all mice. The best and headiest berrybrew is made now and stored away for the high festivals.

SEPTEMBER

25

The story of Elijah and Gladwin Scuttle

On this day, nearly thirty years ago, Elijah Scuttle was carried off by an owl from Fennywolde, but the fieldmouse managed to escape and fell into the River Thames where he grabbed hold of a piece of driftwood but fell into a swoon from the pain of his wounds.

26

In the Vine month which stands for family, it is appropriate to show the Starwife's lineage

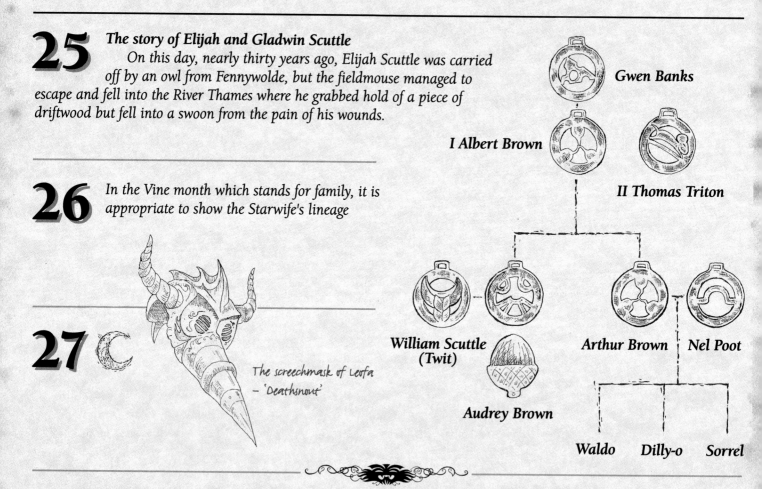

The screechmask of Leofa – 'Deathsnout'

Gwen Banks

I Albert Brown

II Thomas Triton

William Scuttle (Twit)

Audrey Brown

Arthur Brown

Nel Poot

Waldo   Dilly-o   Sorrel

27 ☾

28

The story of Elijah and Gladwin Scuttle

Coming to, Elijah Scuttle paddled the makeshift raft to the bank at Deptford and staggered over land until he collapsed, close to death, in the garden of the old empty house where the two sisters, Arabel and Gladwin, found him and took the poor fieldmouse in.

❧ SEPTEMBER ❧

29 🌰 **The end of the Vine month (squirrel calendar)**

To mark the conclusion of this time, governed by the symbol of the family, this day is set aside for Flouring the Founder, in which the eldest member of a household is covered with flour at noon and must endure the white powder until sun set.

30 🌰 **The beginning of the Ivy month (squirrel calendar)**

A festival time when the majority of squirrel bridings take place.
The making of Ivy Girls and Boys is a customary delight for the youngsters upon this day. These comical figures are then used in contests of marksmanship.
Ivy is the symbol of the royal house of black squirrels who were skilled in the arts of healing. Their realm was destroyed many years ago and all were slain except for two sorely injured soldiers who came to the land of Greenwich, bearing the badge of their Queen as proof of her passing before they too perished. This emblem the present Starwife now keeps.

The badge of the Ivy Realm

OCTOBER

❧ OCTOBER ☙

1 This month is considered to be a ghostly time when the veil between the realm of the living and that of the dead is particularly thin. A mouse prepares himself to encounter anything at this time when the year begins to die.

2 Upon this, the last night to be ruled by the constellations of Mabb, the sleep visitor, take note of your dreams for they are often prophetic.

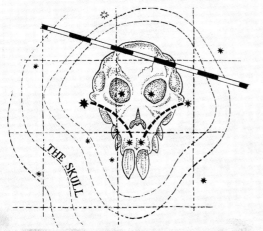

THE SKULL

3 The moon leaves the house of Mabb and enters that of Bauchan, for this is the sign of 'The Skull' (Rat Zodiac)
Ruled by Bauchan, the Skull or 'Headcase' and 'Old Crafty' is a symbol of the god's many disguises and cunning. The rat born now will live by his wits and be an expert liar.
Infamous Headcases include: One Eyed Jake

OCTOBER

4 The most popular past-time amongst the frivolous red squirrel maidens is the divining of future husbands. One method is to take as many apple pips as they have suitors and give each of them a corresponding name. Then, having wet each one, they are placed upon their foreheads until, gradually, they fall off. The last pip to remain will indicate which fellow will prove to be the most faithful and steadfast.

5  Whilst in the sign of the Skull it is an excellent time for examining head lumps.

1 *If this region is well developed it indicates that the rat is mean and cruel*
2 *A sour disposition is shown here*
3 *Cunning and slyness*
4 *Selfishness, brutality and greed*
5 *Faithlessness and deviousness - liable to mutiny*
6 *Cowardly and nervous*

6 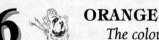 **ORANGE**
The colour signifies prosperity and richness and the actual fruit is a staple ingredient in the mulling of berrybrew which begins at this time.

7 Tonight none other than Orfeo and Eldritch, arrived to speak to the Starwife. They were most solemn and came with dire warnings, for their kind have foreseen a dark time ahead. Before they took to the air they made a point of coming to visit me. With a peculiar look upon their foxy faces they eyed my notes and sketches and asked archly who would be alive this time next year to read it. Their visit has unsettled everyone who dwells beneath the hill, for the Starwife will not say what the bats have told her. Grave tidings I'll be bound.

❧ OCTOBER ❧

8  *About this time, Kempe the pedlar would always arrive in Deptford to deal with Master Oldnose on the all-important business of making mousebrasses. From now on until spring, Master Oldnose would devote himself to this most worthy occupation.*

9 *With windfall apples now rotting upon the ground, the country rats get very drunk from the fermented fruit, so give orchards a wide berth and take no notice of any lewd singing which may come from there.*

10 *The morning mists which rise from ponds and rivers in this hot month are said to carry the spirits of drowned voles and shrews and if you dip your ears into the water you can hear their ghostly voices calling to one another.*

11 *Do not pick blackberries after today for it is well known that Hobb spits upon them and any unwary creature who does so will have bad luck for the rest of his days – or even sicken and die.*

12 The kitten born at this time is called the Blackberry Cat and will be full of devilment, unlike the kitten born in May which is a melancholy creature ill-suited to hunting.

13 *From the writings of the alchemist Dr Elias Theophrastus Spittle:*

The Opal adheres to this month like pox patches to the fawning faces of those dotards at court. Ware this stone, tis filled with ill luck and misfortune save for those born at this time. Such is the lore surrounding this gem that, despite its undoubted loveliness, I have never so much as touched one.

14 Old Todmore's weather wisdom:

In Autumn if the leaves don't fall
The Winter'll be wet for all.

15

The time of the horrendous Rat Kickabout.

In former times when the rats of Jupiter were numerous and much feared, they would play a wild and barbaric sport upon this day. Through the labyrinthine sewers two opposing teams would rampage, each trying to gain control of a very special and gruesome 'ball' – the head of some unfortunate victim – mouse, squirrel, weasel – even one of their own kind, it did not matter. To reach the other side's 'nest' was the only rule and many tackles were decided with the aid of a peeler. Of course it always plunged into anarchy with numerous other 'balls' coming into play – but this only served to make the hellish game more exciting for those awful brutes.

16

Cradle Wake

This strange vigil is only observed by voles. Upon this night they decorate an old, much-used cradle with late flowers and greenery, then by the light of a single candle wait until the dawn – rocking the crib continually. It is said that if they fail to do this then the community will dwindle and the settlement become deserted within the space of three years.

❧ OCTOBER ❧

17 **Taken from the Diary of Walter Thistlewick:**

Today was the October sword dance and because Freddy Beechnut is off my paws at last, Herbert Chickweed's leg being fair mended. All went swimming to start with, when clammity struck. That prize juggins Freddy Beechnut yelled out, just as we were doing the trickyest bit of 'forming the star' with the swords. Well that only puts old Percy off who misses his step and falls crash wallop to the ground, knocking Herbert over as he goes. Up flew their swords, one of them shaving off every whisker on the right side of my face before whipping off Barney's beard! To top it all though, Herbert's only gone and broke his other leg when Percy fell on it.

18 Tonight I was to meet with Dodder, as I received a hastily scribbled note telling me that he had some important information for me. But I waited at the usual spot for over an hour and there was not one sign of him. I do hope nothing has happened to the old fellow.

19 Cats are very good creatures for predicting the weather. If you espy one washing its ears it is sure to rain, if it is scurrying wildly then a wind is due and to see it warm its back to the fire is a sure sign of frost.

20 Time for all creatures to start laying in a plentiful store of fuel for the coming winter.

21  Today I chanced to bump into Pirkin Gim-Gim, I tried to avoid him but to no avail. The hedgehog appeared to be most agitated this day, and when I tried to reprove him for doodling on my best parchment he was too concerned with his own troubles to take any notice. I did learn one thing from his fervid jabbering however, and I don't like it at all. Three nights ago, when I was meant to meet up with Dodder, he saw him in the company of Vinegar Pete and Leering Macky and they were heading for the entrance to the sewers. It did not look as though he went willingly.

---

22 In this the time when chestnuts are plentiful, those maidens of the red squirrels would place two near the fire, naming them after themselves and their sweethearts and watch to see what occurred. If the nuts crackled and flew apart then the courtship would not last, but if they smouldered and burned side by side then that boded very well indeed.

23 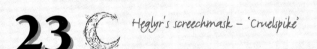 Heglyr's screechmask – 'Cruelspike'

---

24 On this day in 1672 Molly Balker opened an apothecary shop in the City of London.

25

To my great dismay, this morning the body of Pirkin Gim-Gim was found upon the Roman remains in Greenwich Park. The hedgehog had been murdered. The news has alarmed everyone and the Starwife has been besieged with demands for her to uncover the foul assassin and bring him to justice. For myself I am certain that Vinegar Pete and Leering Macky are to blame.

26

The beautiful ginger cat, Imelza, met the mysterious 'Imp' this night in 1664 and so Jupiter, his brother and his sister were conceived.

27

The end of the Ivy month (squirrel calendar)
On this final day a length of Ivy is tied about the corn dolly which has been made out of the last sheaf of the Harvest in order to ensure the indwelling spirit's return to the fields.

28

The beginning of the Reed month (squirrel calendar)
The finest arrows are made from the Reed and so, upon this day, archery contests would be held amongst the squirrels of the old realms. Unfortunately my grey cousins are not very adept with the bow and prefer to shout insults at an enemy from an extremely safe distance.

29

A very eerie night, should both the moon and stars be hidden. Upon Blackheath, countless witnesses have heard a host of phantoms, re-enacting some ancient battle. The chill ring of sword against helm, echoes in the gloom and war cries mingle with disembodied howls of pain. Occasionally figures have been glimpsed, dim and indistinct – yet all locked in a fearful combat. Perhaps in the dawn of days when the Raith Sidhe ruled the land a conflict took place that was so ghastly, its memory was imprinted upon the ether – doomed to be performed at this time throughout the ages. Maybe it is a warning of some kind, or a reminder of ancient horrors.

30

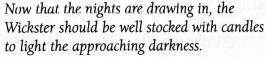

Now that the nights are drawing in, the Wickster should be well stocked with candles to light the approaching darkness.

Rats have no use for candles, preferring instead to burn torches. Madame Akkikuyu however, often made her own, scented versions which she sold to the gullible, claiming they possessed magical properties. This was of course a complete falsehood, as they were often fabricated from nose dribbles, ear scrapings, sewer grease and the jammy goo from between her toe claws! The Green alone knows what was used to give them their undoubtedly startling aromas.

31

It is recorded that Alison Sedge broke the blackened crystal of Madame Akkikuyu upon this day and unwittingly released the spirit of Jupiter.

NOVEMBER

❧ NOVEMBER ❧

1

Extract from the travelling journal of Gervase Brightkin – Day 1

Today the Starwife sent a large troop of sentries into the sewers to find Vinegar Pete and Leering Macky. I was commanded to accompany the grey squirrels as I already have a knowledge of the sewers, but I am far from happy about this and wish I could have stayed behind.

2

Arthur Brown, the brother of our Starwife, was born this day to Gwen and Albert. Although his flame will forever be diminished in comparison to the brilliance of his sister, Arthur has achieved a great deal also. Not content with life aboard the Cutty Sark, it was he who led a company of mice through the sewers to the deserted underground realm of Holeborn in the City which he now rules as Thane.

3

The ideal time for mice to make Pranking Toffee for tomorrow. Also known as 'Rat-choker' and 'Toothgloo'.

❧ NOVEMBER ❧

4 Prank Night

This night the youngsters are allowed a measure of indulgence as they rampage around, causing as much mischief as possible. It is a time to dare others into impish deeds and laugh at the consequences. In The Skirtings, the usual challenge was to sneak into the cellar and write something cheeky near the Grill. Since then the dares have not seemed so dangerous, although last year a young mouse was goaded into climbing the central mast of the Cutty Sark to hang a pair of Mrs Chitter's bloomers upon the rigging.

5 Burning the Bogie

The time when the effigies of enemies or merely those who are resented are paraded from door to door before being sat atop a bonfire and ceremoniously set alight. In the past, the Skirtings mice would always make an image of Master Oldnose. Now however, the youngsters love to make an effigy of Jupiter although some of the older mice cling tightly to their brasses as the fire is lit.

6 Extract from the travelling journal of Gervase Brightkin - Day 6

A new horror has been discovered down in the sewer darkness. I recognised the very spot which led to the pagan temple of the Raith Sidhe — and so we entered.

There, in that Green-forsaken hole, lying across the altar of Mabb, with a spear in his old ribs was the body of poor old Dodder. Of Vinegar Pete and Leering Macky there was no sign, but none of us tarried there and left very swiftly. Who can say what will happen now? After all these years another sacrifice has been made in the temple of the unholy three.

7

In 1664, on this day, the funeral took place of Master William Godwin's family, who had all died of the smallpox.

❧ NOVEMBER ❧

The scuttles

8 ***The story of Elijah and Gladwin Scuttle***
Elijah having been nursed back to health, and being hopelessly in love with Gladwin and she with him, the pair of them eloped from Deptford upon this day and began the journey to Fennywolde where they would remain for the rest of their lives.

9 In the time of the Reed month the best music is usually composed, for now the new reed pipes are cut and made.

10 Kempe the trader was killed on this day by the spirit of Jupiter.

11 Last year at this time Arthur Brown and his wife Nel were further blessed by the arrival of a daughter. Named Sorrel, she is a pretty little thing as my sketch of her when she was only a few months old testifies.

NOVEMBER

12  *According to Legend, the spirit of the Green barricaded himself within the Orchard of Duir upon this day when the first winter came.*

13 *In 1664 William Godwin set off for London to meet with his mysterious uncle, accompanied by his late father's good friend John Balker, the miller, whose fondness for ale proved their downfall.*

14 **Widdershins Eve, or Upside Down Day**
A curious custom of uncertain origin which is followed only by voles. Upon this day all things are performed in reverse. Supper replaces breakfast and the daily chores are done at nightfall. Any articles of clothing must be worn backwards and greetings are changed to farewells.
To meet any vole this day is most confusing as it is impossible to tell whether they are coming or going so it is best to leave them alone.

15 *William Godwin and the miller arrived this night in London but spent too long in 'The Sickle Moon' where Mr Balker became drunk. Upon leaving they were set upon by two rogues who callously murdered the unfortunate miller. Will was saved by the intervention of Doctor Spittle who took the boy in and set him to work in an apothecary shop.*

✤ NOVEMBER ✤

16 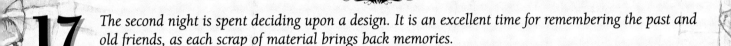 ***The beginning of the four-day quilt festival***
At this time of year, the mice of the Skirtings would gather together and make quilts for the coming winter. On the first night everyone brings out the bags of scraps which they have saved from discarded garments throughout the year and the trading with others begins.

17 The second night is spent deciding upon a design. It is an excellent time for remembering the past and old friends, as each scrap of material brings back memories.

18 Now the sewing begins in earnest, but into some quilt patches small charms are placed; perhaps a sprig of Rowan to ward off evil, a sachet of salt to break any spells that may be cast over the sleeper, a pawful of rosemary to keep nightmares at bay and a small piece of iron or silver for good luck.

19 The last night of the quilting festival is spent putting on the final touches. Only when all are finished can the merrymaking commence and the first dance is always performed upon the new, laid out bedspreads.

NOVEMBER

20 Sad tidings. The news reached me that Jacob Chitter, Oswald's father died on board the Cutty Sark this very morning. The poor fellow has never been the same since the loss of his son, what will his widow do now? No doubt Gwen Triton will take care of her, but she already has her paws full seeing to the wants of the drunken midshipmouse.

21 **From the writings of the alchemist Dr Elias Theophrastus Spittle:**

Here doth the Topaz find itself. This jewel may protect the wearer from the effects of poison, yet little evidence of this did I find when I ate of a Dutch Pudding that had gone a–mouldering. For three days I did have the gripe in mine stomach and was forever on the pot being tortured in the bowels most cruelly.

22 **Nepwort Day**
Named in the memory of young Henry Nepwort who was caught in a November gale whilst out collecting firewood and was whisked away by a sudden, ferocious gust, never to be seen again. No mouse would ever tempt fate by searching for fuel this day, especially if the wind is from the North.

NOVEMBER

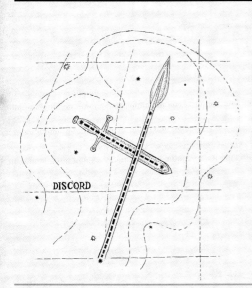

DISCORD

23  **_The moon enters the sign of 'Discord' (Rat Zodiac)_**
Also called 'The Big Brawl' and 'Kill'ems'. Bauchan
is never happier than when sowing disharmony
amongst others. His shameless lies were responsible for many wars in the
beginnings of time and so the rat born now will also be a liar, yet also
argumentative and quick of temper. It is said that a Brawler has many friends,
all dead. Should the stars blaze in a clear sky tonight, it is a sure signal that
there will be murder a-plenty this month.
Infamous Brawler Rats include: Black Ratchet
Mouldtoes
Clunker

24  **_The end of the Reed month (squirrel calendar)_**
As most thatches were traditionally made of Reeds, it is well to check that all roofs are secure and
can withstand the coming winter storms.

25 **_The beginning of the Elder month (squirrel calendar)_**
An unlucky tree closely linked with witches. It was
widely believed in early times that rat-hags used to ride
through the air upon Elder twigs to the hideous revels of Mabb. Especial
care must be taken during this time to ensure that herbs of virtue and
talismans of good fortune are in their proper place within the home to keep
out any unwelcome enchantments.

NOVEMBER

26 Now that the days are turning cold and prey is difficult to find, a rat must sharpen his fangs and practise the devilish skills of capture and murder.

27 **Taken from the Diary of Walter Thistlewick:**

We of the Skirting's Morris and Sword Dancers have never been so mortifide as today.I'd made it my business to make sure Freddy Beechnut practised his steps for 'Wave in Winter'. Anyway there we was all dressed up in our tatting suits, waitin to leap in and do our capers, when the tune suddenly starts and lo and behold if a group of mousewives haven't set up on their own and were already waving there hankies about. Seems we've made such a mess of things this past year, we've been ousted. Mousewives doing the Morris – it's just not right! I was so upset I blew my nose on both my wavy hankies then snapped my tiddling wand.

28 Beware of chilblains in the cold winter.

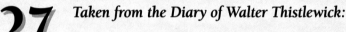

29 The Sign of the Fieldmouse

The most respected of all country brasses, this is worn only by those mice who truly love the land and whose hearts are filled with wonder at the everyday magic of growing things. Master William Scuttle and Woodget Pipple could have borne no other symbol.

30 Orace Day

The sole occasion when a rat turned his back on his race's beliefs and traditions to listen to the teachings of the Green, is commemorated today. 'Orace Baldmony was a rat of the sewers who rebelled against the cruel world of Jupiter and his fellow creatures in the year 1789. In those days the ancestors of the Deptford Mice lived in the cellar of the house as it was not then deserted and the Grill had not become an entrance to terror. When 'Orace appeared, he was greeted kindly and taught the ways of the Green Mouse. But Jupiter sent a gang of the fiercest rats in pursuit and so the first mice of that place were killed and 'Orace's head was impaled upon a spike. The Lord of the Sewers then placed an enchantment upon the Grill to punish the mice who had harboured his mutineer and ever afterwards the dark magic would send helpless victims trotting down to their doom.

A rather peculiar carving of Orace Baldmony executed by an ancestor of Master Oldnose

DECEMBER

DECEMBER

1 A sleepless night

Never have I known such a night of storm, the gales howl about the observatory hill. Even down in my quarters I can hear the violence of the squall and can only pray that all folk are safely by their hearths.

2 A day of portent

The Great Oak is no longer standing — the gales have torn it up by the roots and flung it down the hillside. Many are reading this as a very ill omen and I even heard several murmurs against the Starwife — muttering that she is to blame because she is merely a mouse. One of the leaders of this discontent was none other than Fitz, her very own attendant.

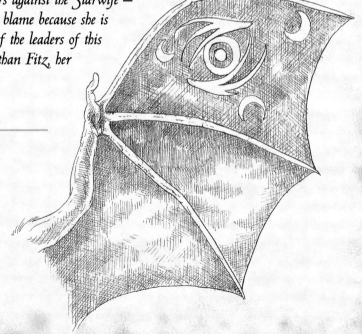

3

Tonight those bat weanings who, throughout the year have studied the ways of their elders and passed the many trials and tests, become Moonriders. Singing the plainsong they have learned, they take to the air in formation with their wings painted with the sign of the eye and remain aloft until the moon begins to set.

❧ DECEMBER ❧

4 The robin is now a frequent visitor to gardens. It was the robin who bore the sacred flame of making from the Green's own forge, to that of Wilfrid the smith but in so doing was scorched and died shortly after. To honour this valiant deed, the Green commanded that the little bird's descendents would bear the noble scorchmark ever afterwards upon their breast.

5 ### Rough Noise Day

If an individual, or indeed a whole family has been behaving rudely or constantly upsetting others throughout the year, this is the time to tell them. Ringing bells and shouting a list of the offending faults, the community march three times around the boundaries ending up at the nuisance's door where the shamed miscreant must apologise and promise to mend his ways.

6 ### From the writings of the alchemist Dr Elias Theophrastus Spittle:

The Turquoise, being a most harmonious and pretty jewel, is linked to the month of December. One of the most useful of gems to keep in an amulet, it doth change its colour when danger approaches or when illness is near. Hence do I find this stone to bring much comfort for I study it noon and night and never yet has it chanced to dim or vary its hue.

7 When the snow and ice comes to Greenwich, it is usual for those who live beneath the hill to hold a 'Frost Fair' upon the frozen pond. These glacial galas boast skating contests, sledging down the observatory hill and there are always plenty of roasted chestnuts and steaming bowls of mulled berrybrew to go round.

DECEMBER

8 The night when Thomas Stubbs and Woodget Pipple ventured into the haunted barn at Betony Bank, where Thomas encountered the ghost of a young mouse who had been murdered there many years earlier.

9 **Birtle's Day**
The feast day of Birtle Whitlow, a weasel who was martyred for his belief in the Green by a mob of bloodthirsty, Hobb-worshipping crows, who pecked out his eyes before carrying him off to devour him in the tree tops. He is the patron of all creatures afflicted with blindness or any disorder of the eye.

Teased for being an albino, Oswald Chitter often prayed to Birtle in the hope of making his pink eyes become 'normal'.

10 Mistletoe has many uses, including the divination of buried treasure. The Starwife recalls a conversation she had with Madame Akkikuyu concerning this virtue of the plant.

'Mistletoetoes very magic, my mouselet. It very clever leafy bush. Find riches it can, Akkikuyu know, she try. When sun go down, Akkikuyu hold out green twiggies and go a-looksee. Not far she go when the toetoes jiggle and shake, so Akkikuyu start to dig. Oh what delight she find, a chicken bone and two sucked sweeties. Very lip licky – oh yes.'

11 **A painful day**
I sit here nursing a very sore face. That wretched drunkard Triton actually hit me! I only told him what everyone else has been saying, that he's being a fool and should pull himself together before he drives his long-suffering wife away. I won't begin to set down the names he called me, I pride myself that my pen will never be so degraded, but that's the last time I go to that rotten old ship of his.

12  Keep a watchful eye upon the weather for Old Todmore clearly states:
December's frost and January's flood
Ne'er bode the fieldmouse any good.

13 Heralded by a comet, Jupiter was born this day in 1664.

14 **The Sign of Courage and Bravery**
This rarely bestowed symbol was last awarded posthumously to Oswald Chitter.

15 Legend tells that this is the day when the evil cold finally breached the Green's defences at the Orchard of Duir and he was compelled to take shelter within the branches of an oak tree.

DECEMBER

16

The moon enters the sign of 'The Bluebottles' (Rat Zodiac)

Also known as 'The Swarm', 'Corpse Feasters' and 'The Buzzing Stars'. A rat born in this time will revel in using others for his own gain and gleefully pounce upon those much weaker than himself. As flies dine off decay, so too will the Bluebottle Rat, for his palate will always prefer rotting carrion to fresh meat. Amongst rat society this is a fairly common sign and though it holds no great honour, it is still thoroughly respectable.

Infamous Bluebottle Rats include: Finn

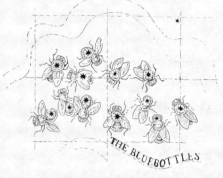

THE BLUEBOTTLES

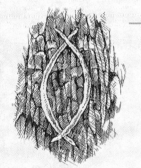

17

(squirrel sign language)

To see this carved upon the bark of a tree, most especially an oak, is always a relief to the wary traveller for this announces he is entering friendly territory.

18

An incredible day.

I can hardly set it down for all the excitement. This very evening, black squirrels arrived in Greenwich! Everyone was amazed, for the last of the race was thought to have died with the old Starwife, but no. They are here, as large as...well, themselves! There are two of them, an older fellow, Modequai, and his daughter, Morella. It is rumoured that they are the sole survivors of the Hawthorn Realm. As soon as they arrived Modequai insisted on seeing the Starwife and, Green to goodness, he has demanded that the Silver Acorn be given to his daughter! The Starwife refused him, but they have been given quarters under the hill, an act which I find most unwise.

Modequai

DECEMBER

19   **SCARLET**

I conclude my discourse on colour with my favourite, not only because I hail from the red branch of squirrels, but also because at this time of year it is so readily found upon the bare hedgerows and Holly trees. Yet this fiery tint is also linked with magic. A ratwitch will always wear something red to proclaim her vocation, Madame Akkikuyu possessed a spotted red shawl for this very purpose and I have heard that in the ancient wildness of Oxleas Wood, a day's march from Greenwich – a certain Nanna Redcap dwells.

20   *Now is the time of the mumming plays*

These ancient dramas stretch far back into myth and the wording is passed down the generations without change. The most common sort is the story of the Green Mouse and his flight into the Orchard of Duir pursued by the forces of Winter, followed by his eventual and victorious re-emergence. More recently, however, the tale of Jupiter has become popular, no doubt the attraction being the cat costume for four mice which I have to admit is quite impressive and always delights the children.

21   *This is the shortest day and the longest night – a time to beware the Midwinter Death, ring all bells to ward Him away, snuggle inside your home and light as many candles as possible.*

22   *Here ends the Elder month (squirrel calendar)*

To burn an Elder branch upon this night will reveal to the brave or foolhardy every Ratwitch or Hobber in the district. Yet to undertake this perilous experiment exposes the curious to great danger, because the worshippers of evil become instantly aware of them also and know that the black secrets of their hearts are laid bare. History records that following this night there have always been many mysterious deaths amongst the stubborn and reckless.

23

A time of watchful unrest for those of the squirrel houses, for this extra day falls between the end of the Elder month and the beginning of the Birch. Because of this, the day is considered to be outside all protection and anything may occur.

Modequai is making himself more popular with each passing day, and discontent with the Starwife is running high. Many are now turning towards Morella, hoping that she will sit upon the Living Throne. Morella is a strange creature, beautiful yet distant, and I wonder why the Starwife tolerates both her and her father's presence. She does however remind me of someone I cannot place and I believe that the Starwife is similarly disturbed by the same troubling thought.

24

The beginning of the Birch month (squirrel calendar)
This is a time for bringing indoors branches of evergreen trees to cheer up the drab winter months. The most common form of decoration is the 'Kissing Bough' - a globe made from holly and ivy, with a sprig of mistletoe hung in the centre. Once this has been suspended from the ceiling of any hole or chamber the custom of kissing any who stand beneath it is expected to be observed – whoever or whatever they are.

25

This most holy day is set down as when the Green Mouse first awakened in Crete in the place which later became the Shrine of Virbius.
To commemorate this, most creatures will feast and give one another small gifts – usually beneath the kissing bough. Candles and incense are always popular presents, as are evergreen garlands, but other trinkets are also exchanged.

DECEMBER

26  *Ratting Day*
At this time the local mousebrass-maker will dress up in a rat costume made from scraps of material, visit every home and pretend to be ferocious until given something small and tasty to eat. Most mice love this quaint old custom and bake little cakes especially for this visitor, but many of the younger ones hide behind their mothers as some Ol' Ratties can be quite frightening.

27 On this night, in the churchyard of St Annes, Will Godwin discovered Imelza and her kittens, Jupiter, Dab and Leech.

28  *Innocent's Day*
In this grim, cold time the mice remember those who have been victims of the peelers and offer prayers up to the Green Mouse to keep their souls by him.

29  *Wassail Night*
The time when the squirrels of every realm would parade in solemn procession to their particular sacred tree and pour libations of bread and ale upon its roots whilst singing the traditional wassailing carol.

> **Wassail wassail, from poor to the crown**
> **Our bread it is white and our ale it is brown**
> **Our bowl it is made of this sacred tree**
> **All are true servants who drink unto thee.**

❧ DECEMBER ℥

30   *A day of revolt*

Supported by a host of my grey cousins, led I might say by Fitz, Modequai barged into the Starwife's chamber and tore the Silver Acorn from about her neck. Then 'The Usurping Mouse' as she was called, was driven away, pelted with empty acorn shells and shot at with arrows. Oh the outrage! The defaming insult! Then did the strange Morella ascend to the Living Throne and the amulet was put about her throat. A black squirrel once more holds the highest office, and now I know why she appears familiar and why the true Starwife delayed any action against her and her scheming father. In her face, Morella is very like the young Alison Sedge. Surely there is some devilment here. **What is to become of us all now?**

31

On this last day of the year and my final entry in this almanack, I must try to look to the future with hope. It is said that the passing year represents an old friend who is giving way to the new infant of tomorrow, how appropriate that belief is now with the Starwife gone. What sinister darkness lies ahead for us all? Audrey Scuttle was placed upon the Living Throne by the Green himself, a madness has consumed the folk of Greenwich and I fear for what will undoubtedly befall them. A dismal, unpleasant place has this become and I shall not spend the eve here!

Farewell now. Oft is it repeated that dire perils and uneasy times unite old enemies. I am now going to prove the truth of it, for I am away to the Cutty Sark – to patch up my quarrels and carouse this darksome night with Thomas Triton.

May the reader of this almanack fare better than I in the days to come. I raise a bowl of Berrybrew in your honour.

May the Green keep you safe
and a
Happy New Year to you all